13-95

An Impossumble Summer

An Impossumble Summer

B. W. Clough

Illustrations by Janet Little

Walker and Company   New York

Copyright © 1992 by B. W. Clough
Illustrations copyright © 1992 by Janet Little

First published in the United States of America in 1992
by Walker Publishing Company, Inc.

Published simultaneously in Canada by Thomas Allen & Son
Canada, Limited, Markham, Ontario

Library of Congress Cataloging-in-Publication Data
Clough, B. W.
An impossumble summer / B. W. Clough.
p. cm.
Summary: After years of living abroad, ten-year-old Rianne and her
family move to Reston, Virginia, where the acquaintance of a talking
possum seems to influence the luck in their lives—sometimes for
better and sometimes for worse.
ISBN 0-8027-8150-0
[1. Opossums—Fiction. 2. Moving, Household—
Fiction. 3. Family life—Fiction. 4. Luck—Fiction.] I. Title.
PZ7.C6239An 1992
[Fic]—dc20 91-32451
CIP
AC

Printed in the United States of America

2 4 6 8 10 9 7 5 3 1

To Lesley and Phe,
inadvertent inspiration

An
Impossumble
Summer

1

We hated the house on Hartwick Road the moment we saw it. "It looks like something stamped out by machine," I said, aghast.

"Rianne, if you can't be positive, be quiet," Mom said, in the tone she used when she was at the end of her tether. "Daddy rented this house, and he had more on his mind than architecture."

It was Shannon's day to be an interior decorator. "It's a colonial, but not a very traditional one," she said, nodding judiciously, as if she'd been studying house designs for a decade. Then, in a more seven-year-old way, she added, "The way the roof cuts straight across the front makes the house's face look scowly. The green one on the corner is friendlier, because it has a pointy roof."

We looked at the other one, but it resembled ours almost exactly. All the houses, up and down the street, were basically the same except for a few different colors or roof shapes. Two spindly trees were planted by the road in front of each house, giving the entire street the look of an army on parade.

"Houses don't have faces, runt," Abe said from the

1

front seat. "I can guess who's going to have to keep this driveway shoveled out, come wintertime. You better back down the hill, cabbie."

Abe always thinks he knows everything, because he's a teenager. The taxi's underside scraped the asphalt as we rolled backward down the slope toward the garage. The cabbie muttered something rude and stamped hard on the brakes. We all piled out, but he bent down to inspect the damage to his cab before he would unlock the trunk. Abe's reed-thin torso bent like a folding ruler as he set his precious graphite tennis racket carefully down on the front steps. While he took out the bags Mom paid the cabbie and fished in her big traveling handbag for the key to the front door.

The door was painted dark red to match the shutters. There were two keys, and it took her a long time to figure out how the lock worked. Mechanical things have never been Mom's strong point. Finally the door wobbled open. While Mom struggled to pull the key out of the lock we pushed past her to explore the house.

The first thing that I noticed was the smell. The house smelled musty and unused, like an old suitcase does when you bring it down from the attic and open it. There was a living room with a fireplace full of half-burnt newspapers, and a ratty old sofa upholstered in swirls of faded pink and glaring blue. The dining room had nothing in it but an ugly chandelier, the kind with lights that pretend to be candles. "Colonial style," Shannon said again. The floors were covered with wall-to-wall carpet in a putrid shade of green.

4

The back of the house was better—a big kitchen with sliding doors and a porch outside. There was a dishwasher, but the sink was stacked with dirty dishes, and the pots on the stove were caked with old food. "Well, that shows Dad's settled in," Abe said. "Let's see upstairs—I get first dibs on a bedroom!"

"Do not!"

"No, me!"

Abe is taller and older, but Shannon can wriggle and I have a very solid build, not tall or fat but sort of chunky. If Abe is a greyhound, I'm a bulldog and Shannon is a Pekingese. She and I shouldered ahead of Abe and cut him off at the stairs. We galloped up shrieking, and scattered to grab the best bedroom first. The hall was gloomy because it had no windows, and the doors were all shut. I flung open the nearest one. No good—it was a big bedroom with a double bed, unmade. Dad's pajamas lay where he had stepped out of them, on the sickening green carpet.

Shannon had already thrown open another door, screaming, "This one is mine!" Abe opened a door and found a closet with empty shelves. Quick as a lizard I jerked at another door and dashed in. It was a totally empty bedroom, with two windows that faced the back. Without waiting to see more, I yelled, "This one is for me!"

Out in the hall Abe said grumpily, "Oh well, mine's nearest the stairs." We've moved so often that it's easy to be philosophical about our rooms. With claims staked we could afford to compare our prizes. Shannon and Abe had the two front rooms, which were almost exactly the same size. The bathroom was beside my room, which was a little bigger, and Mom and Dad had the biggest one and their own teeny bathroom, too.

Panting, we trooped back down the stairs. Mom was exploring the fridge, which was full of untouched packages of food and sealed cartons of eggs and milk. The freezer was stacked with hamburger and chicken, all in their original plastic wrappings. Mom has trained Dad to shop, but she's drawn the line at his cooking. I popped open a can of Pepsi, when a horrible thought hit me. "Where are we going to *sleep?*" I cried.

"What was all that galloping and yelling?" Mom returned. "I thought you were fighting over rooms."

"Mom, there are no beds! There's no furniture at all! Didn't you have any beds for us in storage?"

"Of course not, dum-dum!" Abe said, and when I thought a second I realized he was right. Dad works for the U.S. State Department. Mom and Dad were posted to Riyadh, Saudi Arabia, when Abe was just a baby. I was born when we were in Stockholm, and Shannon when we were in Greece. Our last posting was Manila. All these years, while we were overseas, the Buechner furniture was in a warehouse. The folks had never had a chance to buy beds for us in the U.S. I realized it wasn't the house that was musty, it must be that psychedelic sofa. Upholstery like that went out in the sixties.

"Don't worry," Mom said. She took out some packages of pork chops frozen so hard that they clunked when she laid them on the counter. "Daddy bought beds for you all. The store is delivering them this afternoon. And the air freight is here, down in

6

the basement. We can unpack the sheets and towels after lunch, and make the beds as soon as they arrive."

"Let the maid do it," Shannon said.

"Yeah," said Abe. "I want to go to the tennis court."

Mom shut the freezer door. "Now, I want all three of you to listen to me," she began. "We're living in the U.S. now. Life in Virginia isn't going to be like living in Manila. One of the most important parts of it will be Doing Things Yourself."

We could hear the capital letters in her voice. "We can't afford servants here," she continued. "No maids, no cooks, no gardeners. We're all going to pitch in and do the work ourselves."

It was a shocking idea, and we sat stunned into silence. No one had ever heard of such a thing in Manila, for sure.

Mom had phoned out for pizza for lunch. With her thick glasses and soft brown hair fluffed around her head Mom doesn't look very formidable, and she spends so much time reading she doesn't usually act tough, either. Every time she does, we're surprised. We sat meek as mice, eating pizza while she outlined our new daily duties. Everyone would make their own bed each morning, and keep their own room tidy. Abe would mow the lawn, when Dad bought a lawn-mower. I would clear the supper table and put dishes into the dishwasher; Shannon would take the lunch duty. Bathrooms would be scrubbed and rugs vacuumed. Naturally, Mom would cook. That was the only bright spot in the whole horrible schedule, because Mom is good at it. Even our chef in Manila

7

would watch respectfully when "Madame" made a béchamel sauce.

But otherwise we were incredibly depressed. Pizza was still a rare treat but I lost my appetite and passed the last piece to Abe. "And Dad wrote that it would be Reston-peace!" I groaned. "We'll be slaving from dawn till dark, like coolies!"

"Seven is much too young to scrub bathtubs," Shannon sulked. "Besides, I don't know how."

"I'll teach you." Mom was firm. "You've got the whole summer to learn. Don't forget, I'm going to try and finish my master's degree now we're back in the States. I won't have time to wait on you. So come September you had better be pros."

"You mean we'll have to do chores even when school starts?" Abe was horrified. "What about my tennis?"

"You're not going to be another Jimmy Connors, anyway," I said unkindly. "Fifteen is already over the hill, as far as being a tennis star goes."

"Brat," he snarled.

"Pig," I retorted. Mom stared so warningly at us we had to quit.

Mom began the new regime right after lunch by making Shannon throw out the pizza box and clear the pop cans. It doesn't sound like much, but anyone would have thought she was being forced to scrub the floor with a toothbrush. To get away from Shannon's whiny complaints Abe and I went out onto the back balcony. "I guess we're going to have to learn to call it a deck," I said gloomily.

The backyard below us sloped down to some

8

woods. There were two rusty deck chairs near the rail. Abe sat in one, and it sagged so alarmingly that he had to get up again. "Rianne, this is going to be *grim*. We're going to be working like dogs."

"And we don't know anybody here," I said sadly. That's the most hateful thing about moving around. Everyone thinks that living in Asia or Greece must be so romantic and exciting. But every time you move you leave all your friends. "It's only the end of May. We won't meet any kids our age until school starts in September." I thought of the endless, boring weeks to come, and remembered Manila with an aching heart. I'm going on eleven, which is an age where friends are important—we learned it in Sex Education. My class at the International School there was having a pool party this weekend. Everyone would be there but me, stuck in a horrible backwater American suburb like something out of *American Graffiti*. A big tear rolled down my cheek.

Abe muttered something about hanging up his tennis shirts, and went in. He can't bear crying girls. A high overcast hung in the sky, too thin for rain but enough to water down the sunshine. I wondered if the sun ever shone in the U.S.; we had spent the last two weeks with Grandma Makenside in Seattle, where it rains constantly.

Shannon came out, still pouting. "Mom says we have to go downstairs and help unpack the air freight."

"In a minute." I cast around for some way to postpone the work for a second. "Look at those woods, Shannon. Maybe we can explore them."

Shannon brightened. "Maybe we could find a hurt squirrel, or a baby bird that fell out of its nest!" When she isn't rearranging furniture Shannon wants to be a vet. The only books she's read outside of school are the ones by James Herriott.

I could hear Mom calling, "Girls! Abe! Come on!" Groaning, we went inside.

The basement was the creepiest part of the new house. We had never lived in a house with one before. It had one tiny window to illuminate the bare cement walls and floor. A washing machine and a dryer lurked in one corner, and a gas furnace in the other. You had to turn on the light even in the daytime, not a proper light, nor even a bare bulb in a socket, but what Mom called a utility lamp. It looked something like the Statue of Liberty's torch—a bulb in a wire cage, with a hook on one end to hang it by and a handle on the other. A long zip cord plugged it into the electrical socket near the washer.

All the bare essentials for household living had been shipped by air from the Philippines and lay around in big brown cardboard boxes. Abe unfolded the biggest blade on his Scout knife and cut open a box. "Down here is where the ghost lives," he said in a low, thrilling voice.

"The house is less than ten years old," Mom said quellingly. "I'm almost sure this box has towels."

Abe once read us *The Ghost of Canterville Chase* on a long jet flight. He scared us so much we couldn't sleep, and Mom had been furious. But Abe remembers it as one of his crowning achievements as our big brother. So as Mom flipped back in her list, which showed which number box held what, Abe said, "You've studied 'The Cask of Amontillado,' haven't you, Rianne?"

"In school," I said nervously. The tall cylinder of the water heater cast a human-sized shadow on the wall. The utility light was really creepy to use, because its light moved when you moved your hand. The shadows skittered along like live things, especially Abe's long, lean one. This past year he's grown so tall, without getting even a little bit wider, that his head seems slightly too small for his body. His shadow looked like a worm's.

"Well, look! There's where Montresor was bricked in!"

I held the light up to see where Abe pointed. Behind a heap of boxes one portion of the wall was different. It was made of cinderblocks instead of cement. The cinderblock section filled a space as wide as a door from floor to ceiling. It was exactly the way a sealed, secret tomb would look. A cold, crawly feeling trailed down my spine.

"What's Amontillado?" Shannon wanted to know.

"It's a story by Edgar Allan Poe," Abe said, answering her real question. "About a guy who was bricked up in a hole in a basement—alive!"

Shannon's brown eyes were as big as saucers in her little, round face. With exaggerated care Abe tiptoed over and rapped on the blocks with the handle of his knife. They rang hollow! "Oh, my God," I almost whimpered.

"Now Abe, cut that out!" Mom said. "Take this box upstairs and put it by the linen closet."

"But Mom!" Shannon clutched at her sleeve. "Why *is* it cinderblocks just there?"

The expression on Mom's face was so gloriously practical and impatient that I relaxed even before she said, "That's where the fireplace is, up above in the living room."

"Oh! Of course! You'd need a foundation, for the fire-box!" Shannon reverted back to interior decorating again.

"And I guess cinderblock always sounds hollow." I was so relieved I laughed. We must have looked like idiots. Sometimes Abe is really a rat.

2

There must be some secret network among tennis players. In less than a week Abe met and got cozy with three tennis nuts. They needed a fourth for doubles. He played with them every day, and signed up for an August tennis tournament that the county runs.

There wasn't anyone my own age living nearby. School was still in session, and the only kids I saw playing outside were little boys. I was almost sorry that Mom and Dad had decided it wasn't worth starting us in school again for just the last two weeks. There was nothing to do but housework.

The lady next door came by and gave Mom a cake. Her name was Mrs. Hernandez, and she had long hair, perfectly white, flowing down her back over an argyle hand-knit sweater. "My granddaughter will be so glad to meet you when she gets back," she told me, and pinched my cheek with her knobbly knuckles. "Louise is just your age."

That sounded very hopeful. "Where is she?"

"Oh, she and Liane and Joseph—my daughter and son-in-law, you know—are in Venezuela. He's on

13

sabbatical there, writing a book. They'll be back in the fall. I'm just keeping their house for them."

So that was no good. "Maybe I should take up a sport, too," I said, after she left. "Want to go to the pool, Shannon?"

Shannon had borrowed some graph paper from Dad's desk, and was busy trying to draw a floor plan of the house. "You know you'll just get water on your glasses."

"Well, I can't see to swim without them."

"I want to finish this first." Shannon showed me the plan. She hadn't bothered to measure any of the walls, so the rooms and doorways didn't match up well, and some of the corners weren't square.

There aren't a lot of things I'm good at. But I can always think of easier and simpler ways to get things done right. I get that, and a secretive mentality, from Dad. "You should start with the basement," I suggested. "There aren't any interior walls down there. So it would be easier to get the house's basic shape right."

Shannon rolled her eyes at me. "Would you come with me while I do it?"

"Sure."

Neither of us would admit it to each other, and of course we'd both die before letting Abe know, but we were both a little nervous about going into the basement alone. When Mom sent me down to move the laundry from the washer to the dryer, I always invented an excuse to have Shannon come along. And when Shannon had to carry down empty boxes she got me to help carry some. Our family never throws away empty boxes unless they're in tatters. You always need them when you move again.

So we went downstairs together. "If you'd measure the walls you'd be able to get them on paper more accurately," I said.

Shannon sighed. "Daddy won't let me play with his steel tape measure." That was because Shannon had almost cut her arm off with it once, trying to measure a jeep. The end had hooked on the front grille, and when the driver pulled away, the steel strip had tightened around her elbow. Shannon still has a nice scar up her left arm.

"You could pace the distance." For a while I pretended not to look at the cinderblock section. But then it got boring, watching Shannon count her steps. I decided Mom would appreciate it if I stacked up the empty boxes. We had at least thirty, all sizes. I nested little ones the size of an orange crate into big ones made to hold furniture, and lined them up.

"Not against the wall, Ree! I have to pace there."

"Okay, okay!" I stacked them in the middle, making a wall that almost divided the basement.

Suddenly, from beyond the boxes, Shannon gave a yelp. "Ree! Oh, Ree!"

I darted around my homemade wall. When I saw that Shannon was crouched near the cinderblock wall my heart jumped. Then I took hold of myself and came nearer. "What's wrong?"

"There's a hole here! And I fell!"

I squatted down to look. There was a hole in the concrete floor, right up against the cinderblocks, about a foot across. Shannon had stepped right into it. Her foot had gone all the way in to the knee. "Are you stuck? Did you sprain your ankle?"

"I don't know." In the dim light of the utility lamp I could see her lower lip trembling. "I'm scared to pull. I think Amontillado's got me!"

"Oh, for Pete's sake!" I grabbed her bare knee and lifted. Her foot came straight up, with hardly any resistance at all except for where her sneaker scraped against the side. "Dummy! Now, watch where you're going next time!"

"Oh, Ree, thank you!" She bent to look at the hole. "Do you think it's a rabbit hole?"

"In a basement?" I looked, too. It looked like an ordinary dark hole. I went to get the light. The basement ceiling was low enough so that I could unhook it without having to stand on a box. The cord was long enough for me to hold the lamp near the hole. It was still an ordinary hole, about two feet deep. The sides were the rough cement of the floor slab.

I began to move the lamp away, but Shannon said, "Wait! Ree, I see something, down on this side!"

"Here, hold the light and let me kneel where you are." I crouched and looked from Shannon's angle. Sure enough, at the bottom the hole went sideways, tunneling under the floor! "And there's something in it!"

"What? Where?"

"I can't make it out. It looks like a scrap of paper."

"A treasure map—it's a map to an ancient Indian treasure, hidden back in the woods behind the house!"

"Shannon, you make me tired," I said impatiently.

16

"This house was built by developers ten years ago, remember? Why should Ryan Homes put treasure maps in basements?" Then I looked at her sad little face under the bangs, and gave in some. After all, I had nothing better to do. "We can *pretend* it's a treasure map, okay?"

"Oh, yes!"

"Well then, we better get it out so we can start hunting for the gold. Or maybe it'll be just wampum." I began to reach into the hole.

Shannon grabbed my wrist. "Wait a minute. Suppose it's a rat's nest?"

Quickly I snatched my hand back. "You're right—we should look in there first. We need a little mirror, and maybe a stick."

"I'll go borrow Mom's pocket mirror from her purse!"

"And bring the duct tape from the garage," I called after her as she thundered up the stairs. I didn't really like sitting down here alone—by the cinderblock wall, too. But I held onto the rubber handle of the utility lamp and set my teeth. Mr. Amontillado had better not give me any trouble!

Shannon came clattering back. She had forgotten the stick, of course, but I used a strip of corrugated cardboard from a box. It was hard to tape the round hand mirror onto it without blocking most of the surface, and we used rather a lot of duct tape. Then when I stuck it into the hole, Shannon had to hold the lamp at just the right angle, so that its light shone down the side of the hole.

"The map must be painted on birchbark," Shannon said. "What kind of tribe lived around here?"

17

"Chesapeakes, I guess. Or Potomacs. Unless Herndon is an Indian name." It was hard to talk. To jiggle the mirror around I had to lie flat on my stomach on the concrete, and almost hang my head down the hole. When I finally got a good view inside, all my blood seemed to rush suddenly downhill into my head, so that I felt dizzy. I lay without moving or saying anything, while Shannon nattered on beside me.

Then I rolled over. "Here," I said, passing her the mirror. "You have a look."

Shannon took my place, and I held the lamp while she looked. When she raised her head again her round face looked less like a baby's than I had ever seen it. "What *is* it?"

We took turns looking. There was a little chamber hollowed out underneath the floor slab. The room was maybe the size of a small table, though our light didn't quite shine that far. And it was *furnished*. The dirt floor was covered with a rug pieced out of old postage stamps. The dirt walls were papered with sections of the *Reston Times*. There was a bed the size of a big book, tidily made up in a cardboard Christmas gift box from Hecht's, and covered with a red bandanna coverlet.

"A pixie," Shannon breathed. "Our house has an elf!"

"Or talking mice," I suggested. "Like Miss Bianca."

"But where is it?"

There was no sign of recent occupation. All we could smell, when we sniffed deeply, was a damp

18

basement smell. Something about the neatly made bed suggested that whoever had lived under our basement no longer did so.

Emboldened, I reached in and groped around with one hand. But the depth of the hole made it impossible for me to force my elbow around the bend. "You try, your arm's shorter," I said. Shannon lay down and stuck her arm in. "Don't pull at the rug. The hobbit, or whatever it is, might not want his hole all messed up."

"Here—this was right by the door in the corner." It was an old can I had not seen, from tuna fish or cat food, the most unelfin souvenir you could imagine. There was nothing in it. Shannon reached in again and fumbled around.

"Girls! Are you down there?" Dad was calling from the top of the basement steps.

"Yes, Dad!" I yelled back. "I'm helping Shannon make a floor plan."

"Well, wind it up, will you? It's almost time to set the table."

"We'll only be a minute." I heard him shut the door again. "Hurry up, Shannon!"

"Here's that paper you saw." She fished it up between two fingers, and I stuck it in my shorts pocket to look at later. "And I can just snag that coverlet. Shall I?"

"Yes. But do it carefully." I wanted one genuinely miniature item to examine upstairs in broad daylight, just to prove we weren't dreaming. Shannon dragged the coverlet up, and it was perfect—not an ordinary plain bandanna, but two kerchiefs, a red and a blue one, quilted together to enclose something soft. "All *right!* Now come on, or Mom will be after us!"

In our excitement we wolfed our food, and got a head start on the dishes while Mom and Dad were still eating. In fact, I snaked his plate away almost before Dad put his knife and fork down on it. "Hey, what's the rush?" he demanded.

"Uh—" A lot of original but unlikely stories spun through my mind: we were having a race; Shannon wanted to watch an animal program on TV; I was hungry for dessert. But these smoke screens never fool Dad. He works in security for the government, setting up metal detectors in embassies, and so on. We kids aren't supposed to know that there's a locked cabinet bolted to the back wall of his closet, behind the tie rack, to hold his guns. Dad is tall and square and wide, like a blond brick—the absolute last person in the world to discuss elves with. He's pretty good at inventing plausible cover stories, though, and smelling out implausible ones, too. So I made mine as ordinary and boring as I could. "We want to look over Shannon's paint chips while there's still daylight. She's going to turn the basement into a rec room."

Shannon picked up the cue fast. "Yeah, Dad. Can I put up drywall? We could paint it pink. Wood paneling is so tacky and old-fashioned."

"Sure, buttercup. Just don't spend more than your allowance, okay?" He laughed, and rumpled her hair. Shannon has redecorated every one of our houses with nothing but pure imagination. Mom and Dad would never consider doing it for real. For one thing it would cost millions of dollars. Shannon has incredibly ex-

20

pensive taste in furniture. Besides, we move too often. We hurried upstairs to her room and dumped out her shoebox of paint samples onto the bed. Then we sat on the floor and looked over our trophies.

The tin can was unimpressive. The label, if it had ever had one, was gone. The inside didn't smell of anything in particular when I sniffed it. The top had been taken off with a can opener. It could have held anything.

The coverlet, though, was exciting. Its red and blue bandannas were old and faded. Their edges weren't properly sewn together, but just coarsely laced with what looked like horsehair. I peeked in between the big crude stitches and used a pencil point to tease out some of the stuffing. "What is it, fur?" Shannon breathed.

I laid the tuft onto a paint sample and poked at it. "No—it's dandelion seeds, see?" I let her hold it while I wrote that down. Daddy says it's important in an investigation to keep good records.

"And what about the paper? Is it a map?"

I took it from my pocket and smoothed it. It was an old, waterstained advertising leaflet for the Pet Farm Park. "That's right here in Reston," I said thoughtfully.

"Why do pets need a farm?" Shannon wanted to know. "Do they grow dog food and cat food?"

"I don't think it's for pets like that," I said. "I guess it has goats and rabbits and stuff, for people to pet." I peered at the blurry lettering, which was just barely readable. "It's open in the summer. I wonder if Dad would let us go?"

21

3

I worried about getting to the Pet Farm for a few days before asking Dad. But he surprised me by saying yes right away. "And here's some money to get you in," he said. "I appreciate the time you're spending amusing your little sister, Rianne. That's not always fun for a big girl like you."

I felt so guilty that I almost blurted out the whole story right there. But it's so difficult to say things. Mom says I'm like an onion, all the layers tightly hugging themselves. So I mumbled something or other, and didn't go into details.

The sea freight had come at last, all our clothes and books and toys and furniture. Our bicycles came too, and Mom made Abe assemble them for us. So we were able to ride to the Pet Farm Park in style.

As we coasted down into the parking lot Shannon squealed, "Look! A lion cub!"

She jumped off her bike. Sure enough, a fat, sandy-colored cub was scuffling around in the azalea plantings. The man holding the leash even let Shannon pet it, very carefully, while I locked our bikes together onto the rack. "I'm going to like this place," Shannon told me.

We bought our tickets and went in. Right away I realized why Dad had complimented me. School was just out, and the place was swarming with kids, little ones—from tots sucking their thumbs up to six- and seven-year-old monsters. There was a long barn, some fenced enclosures, and two ponds with monkeys on the islands in the middle.

Shannon forgot all about the search for an animal that might have lived under our basement. She ran to stroke the big Galapagos tortoises in their pen. I followed her around, not having any real idea what I was looking for myself. Most of the books about smart animals involve mice, but I had read *Watership Down* last spring, and thought rabbits would be a possibility.

In a babyish sort of way it was fun to feed the ponies cracked corn, and pet the goats and piglets, who would nuzzle right up to you for attention. But no one older than eight would call it exciting. We threw alfalfa pellets to the ducks, and Shannon decided to be a vet again. Then the hay wagon drew up to haul the kids around the pasture to see the buffalo and the antelope. "You go on," I told Shannon. "Hay makes me sneeze."

When the wagonload of shrieking kids trundled off I watched the swans and geese for a while. Then, bored, I wandered around the barns again. The crowd was worse than ever, all waist-high or lower, except for the occasional parent. The llamas were the most fun, I decided. I wondered if one could live comfortably on our deck.

23

Around behind the llama pen I found another little display area. It was devoted to local animals. The nook was quite empty, probably because the animals were wild, locked in cages rather than loose for petting. A raccoon slept in a box, three squirrels raced around on their branches and exercise wheels, and a red fox looked at me with a complete lack of interest. There were a lot of empty cages. I sat down on one with a sigh; the quiet was a relief.

"Aha," said a small, rusty voice behind me. "You live at 10121 Hartwick Road."

"I do?" I did. I glanced wildly around.

"And you've been in the basement there."

Oh, my God, I thought, it really is an elf! "Won't you come out so I can see you?" I quavered. "Are you—dangerous or anything?"

"You can read about how dangerous I am on the label," said the rusty voice very grumpily. "Right there, by your knee."

I bent and peered into the lower cage. It seemed empty, but hanging on it was a sign like other signs in the Pet Farm, describing the habits and features of the animals. This one said, "OPOSSUM (*Didelphis virginiana*), a common animal in the eastern United States. Mr. Opossum lives in a tree. He sleeps in the daytime. He eats leaves and bugs." And it was illustrated with a small line drawing.

I read it over very slowly, twice, like a robot stuck in a groove, and was halfway through a third reading when the straw at the back of the cage rustled. I tensed, ready to jump back if something lunged at me.

But it really was an opossum. Its fat, bandy-legged

24

OPOSSUM (*Didelphis Virginiana.*)

A common animal in the Eastern United States.

Mr. Opossum lives in a tree. He eats leaves and bugs.

body was about a foot and a half long, and covered with sparse gray and white bristly fur. It had little reddish eyes and a long, pointed pink snout. I had never seen one before, but when I glanced at the drawing on the label the resemblance was good. They were extraordinarily ugly and uncuddly animals. "Say something more," I said, incredulous.

" 'Say something more,' " the opossum mimicked me sarcastically. "That's all people are interested in. Talking. Yap, yap, yap. Any other interesting or useful quality I possess might as well be cicada hulls and dry leaves."

"You do interesting things?" I asked, my mind still full of elves and fairies. "Wishes, and such?"

"Wouldn't you like to know," the opossum snarled. "I've learned how to deal with people. Do what I want, and then I'll do what you want—maybe."

Perhaps I had spoken rather rudely. "Tell me what you want, and I'll be happy to try," I said. "I didn't mean to sound grabby. Not all people are like that, you know. I was just a little surprised."

"Well, I am an unusual animal," the opossum allowed. "You can take that lock off the cage door. I want to go home."

"And you live at *my* house?"

"Ugh, never! That prison! I was jailed there, incarcerated for almost a year! No, I want to go back to my tree."

"Your tree," I repeated, bemused. It was true, no one would live under a basement slab by choice.

"Of course I live in a tree—read the sign! It's an oak, away behind your house, a stump actually. Now open that lock!"

"Um—" I don't think a little creative lying does much harm, but lock breaking is a crime. "Even if I could break it, which I doubt, wouldn't it be stealing? You belong to the Pet Farm."

The opossum rolled its ruby eyes. "I do not! I'm a wild animal!"

"I'm sure they have a permit, or whatever it is, to keep you," I said. "Now, if I knew the circumstances—"

"So that's what you want?"

If it wanted to bargain, I could bargain. "If that's what you've got."

The opossum scratched its head with one pale paw. "I'd rather give a bit of luck," it muttered. "My story is my own business."

That made me laugh. "Mr. Opossum, you aren't a leprechaun in disguise, that's impossible."

"Mister, indeed! Call me Impossumble, if you must, and that's Ms.!" It, or rather she, held onto the cage wire with her front paws and peered nearsightedly at me. "And I'm talking to you, aren't I? I got you to come here, and recognized the smell of my cave on you, did I not? If that's not already impossum-ble, what is?" She made a few cackling, rusty creaks that I realized were opossum laughter.

"Story first," I said firmly. "I can't free you unless you convince me it's right."

"I'm so glad I'm an animal," the Impossumble sniffed. "Without all these moral scruples. Well! I live in a tall tree stump in the woods. One day last spring a little boy caught me in a box trap. He kept me in his basement because—" She stopped.

27

"Because of the luck?" I suggested.

"Oh, well!" The Impossumble seemed bitterly resigned. "Yes, that's right. But I fixed him." She grinned, baring a mouthful of sharp little white teeth. "He had to move away. But instead of letting me go, he brought me here."

"That doesn't sound very fair," I agreed. "It's not as if you were born to captivity. And I suppose the Pet Farm could always find another opossum if it wanted to."

"Oh, they're as common as field mice around here, the ordinary ones," the Impossumble assured me. "I'm the only one of *me*, you see—quite an endangered species. Now, hurry up with that lock! Someone might come in any minute!"

I looked at it. It was an ordinary padlock, obviously meant to keep prying tot hands out of the cage. But I had no key. Daddy could have done it, but the lock was too stout for me to just twist off. The cage was welded together out of thick, shiny steel wires, the way dog cages are. "I don't know," I said, shaking the bars. "How do they clean it?"

She scuffled in the straw on the floor. "They tip the cage and slide the floor away."

"Ah!" Of course an opossum wouldn't realize what this meant. I felt around at the side of the cage until I found the latch that secured the bottom. It was nothing but a sliding bolt. The cage was designed to be lifted off its floor for cleaning. "There you are! If I just lift it here at the corner, you can crawl out."

The Impossumble hurried to do so. Before I could lower the cage down again she leaped to the area doorway. "I'm a wild animal," she warned. "You try to jump on me, and I'll bite!"

"I wouldn't do that," I said, stung. The little pink snout wrinkled doubtfully, but she did not run away. I wanted to show her that people aren't all as horrible as she thought. "If you'd like a ride back to Hartwick Road, you could come with us," I said. "We came by bicycle. You could sit in the basket. It doesn't have a lid. Any time you felt nervous you could just jump out and run away."

"I might use a lift." The Impossumble thawed a little.

"Our bikes are out front, near the cars," I said. "Take me up on it or not, whatever you like. I have to pick up my sister, so you can meet us there." She backed warily away as I stepped out. I was careful to walk toward the llama pen without looking back. An attitude of anxious helpfulness would just make her more nervous. Perhaps she was grumpy because it was daytime. I remembered the sign had said that opossums are night animals.

The hay wagon was just coming to a halt beyond the big barn. Children swarmed off it and ran shouting up the hill. Shannon trotted up with sunburn on her nose and straw in her brown hair. "We saw a baby buffalo!" she announced. "It was all brown and plush, like a stuffed toy. And some antelope, and a deer—"

I let her natter on as we walked back through the park. It was after four now, and people were starting to leave. It occurred to me that the Impossumble might have problems getting to our bikes quickly, with everyone pouring through the parking lot. "Let's sit down, Shannon," I said, pointing at the picnic area. "I have a story to tell you."

As I recounted my talk with the Impossumble, Shannon's mouth slowly sagged open. "You're making it up, aren't you," she said when I had done. "It's all pretend. Like the treasure map."

"Shannon, you saw that little bed under the basement as well as I did," I said crossly. "This is real!" When she set her jaw and frowned doubtfully at me, I added, "Well, come on out to our bikes, then—you'll see!"

We went through the gift shop and out into the parking lot without speaking, and I had a moment of doubt, myself. But then my heart gave a tremendous squeeze in my chest. There was a large paper bag from McDonald's in my bicycle basket that hadn't been there before. The clever Impossumble had disguised herself.

I grabbed Shannon's arm. "Now, we're not going to talk about it where people can hear," I cautioned. "No squealing, no exclamations, no questions—you hear? We'll ride quietly home first."

We came up to our bikes and unlocked them. As she bent down to pull the chain free, Shannon shot a quick sideways glance into the bag. She pressed her lips tightly together and nodded at me. We hopped onto our seats and pedaled off.

The bag gave a few alarmed rustles. I set a slow pace so as to give my passenger a smooth ride. Ahead of me, Shannon kept looking back. It seemed like years before we coasted down our own driveway. The moment I stopped, the Impossumble scrabbled out of her bag and down to the ground. She darted behind an azalea bush. "Oh!" Shannon breathed. "Make it talk, Rianne, please?"

"Aren't you going to say thank you?" I said, indignantly.

The Impossumble's pointed snout just poked out from beneath the leaves. "I'll give you a dab of luck instead. You'll like it better."

Shannon squealed with excitement. "Don't you want to live in our basement again?"

I shook my head vehemently at her. The Impossumble's eyes glinted redly above her snout. "No! And furthermore, if you ever suggest it again, I'll— I'll fix you the way I did that Canfield boy."

Shannon isn't good at even broad hints. "How?"

"His parents got a divorce," the Impossumble said, grinning evilly. "Bad luck for him, huh?"

Both Shannon and I were horrified that such a thing was even possible. Divorce was something that happened to other people's parents, usually on TV or in movies. What if the Impossumble began to play tricks on Mom and Dad? "We would never think of it," I said hastily. "Shannon only wondered if you might not want your coverlet back. It's so warm looking, and nicely made, that it'd be cozy come winter."

"I might," the Impossumble said in a surprised tone. "And as for your bit of luck—you don't bet at race tracks, do you, or go to casinos?"

"Of course not," Shannon said.

"There aren't any within fifty miles of here," I added.

"Oh, well! Go downtown and buy a D.C. Lottery ticket, then." And with that curt advice the Impossumble slipped away deeper into the brush.

4

For a few days Shannon and I did nothing about the lottery idea. Terrified by the Impossumble's threat, Shannon clung to Mom and Dad whenever they were together. "Have you been telling the girls ghost stories again?" Dad finally asked Abe.

"Of course not!" he denied, justifiably indignant. "I've been working on my serve!"

For my part, I decided to find out about the people who used to live here, just to check on the Impossumble's powers. I made some peanut butter cookies and, before Abe ate them all, took a plateful next door to old Mrs. Hernandez.

"Aren't you sweet!" she thanked me. "Come in, and we'll sit on the deck and have a cup of herbal tea."

She sat with her back against the railing, so that her snowy white hair trailed down into space like Rapunzel's. Most people with superlong hair have to pin it up or braid it or something to get by. I could tell Mrs. Hernandez hardly ever had to go through a revolving door or ride in convertibles. I had to listen to a lot of her personal stuff, how she lived with her daughter's

32

family, how she missed the grandchildren, how she worried about burglars or fire or trees falling down.

"See that big dead one over there?" Mrs. Hernandez pointed over the railing at a tall, leafless trunk. "Sometimes at night I jump awake, thinking that it's come, crash! onto the roof." She fluttered her bony hands, miming the crash and the rattling of roof shingles.

But there wasn't anything she didn't know about the neighborhood. The DeConcinos—that was her daughter Liane's family—bought this house new from the builders, and had seen the neighborhood develop from what was practically wilderness. The big forest behind our houses, for instance, was doomed. "They'll bulldoze it and build cluster houses," Mrs. Hernandez grumbled. "I guess Liane should be grateful it won't be a shopping center!" And she knew a whole saga about the Canfields, though I could tell she thought I was too young to hear all the gory details. Little Bobby Canfield had been learning disabled. The parents had "fought like cat and dog," Mrs. Hernandez remembered. "Finally she left, and took the boy with her. Canfield had to pack everything up himself, when he moved away."

"Where did they go?"

Mrs. Hernandez shrugged her lean shoulders. "A sad business, but that's modern marriage for you. Now remember, you do better when it's your turn!"

When Shannon learned what the Impossumble had done to Bobby Canfield she insisted that we carry the little coverlet down into the woods right away. "And what else should we bring?" she asked anxiously. "I bet she would like a present." We decided on a few apples.

33

The woods in back are owned by the town. A little Reston-maintained trail threaded through the trees and ended at a set of monkey bars. Beyond was unbroken forest. We floundered through the underbrush and scratched our legs on brambles until we were thoroughly discouraged. The ground sloped down and down, growing wet and boggy. No breeze stirred in the valley. Somewhere around here was where the developers planned to build the new cluster houses. The muggy heat made the sweat run down our faces. "I'm tired," Shannon began to whimper.

"I guess we'll have to leave the stuff," I said, defeated. "There must be acres of forest back here. And I wouldn't know an oak stump unless it had acorns on it."

We laid down the little coverlet and the apples on the bole of a huge fallen tree, and then sat on it to rest. But the mosquitoes drove us up the hill and out again to the trail, and so back home.

"You know," I remarked one evening at dinner, "we've been here for almost a month, and we haven't seen the Washington Monument."

"I have," Abe said, chewing. Mom and Dad had brought us to Washington eight years ago, but only Abe had been old enough to really remember it. "It's overrated. What I'd like to see is the Air and Space Museum." He helped himself to another monster portion of mashed potatoes, and sloshed the gravy on with a generous hand. My brother is walking proof that life is unfair. He eats like a pig and stays as slim as a stick. People like me, on the other hand, just look at food and get wider.

"Is it true about the big elephant at the Natural History Museum?" Shannon demanded of Dad. "That it's the biggest stuffed one in the *world?*"

"I think so," Dad said. He looked at Mom. "What do you say, Irene? A family consensus seems to be emerging here."

"We haven't done anything as a family for a while," Mom said.

That was Thursday. On Saturday morning we all piled into the car and drove into the city. Washington is much cleaner and less crowded than the towns in Southeast Asia. When I remarked on it, Dad said, "Wait until you see New York City!" We drove from the Lincoln Memorial up to the Capitol, gawking at the sights. Then we parked and waited in line to get up into the Washington Monument. The view was wonderful, laid out below like a marvelous map.

We ate lunch in an underground restaurant between two of the art museums. It had a waterfall that flowed from a fountain up above down behind a thick sheet of glass that formed one side of the restaurant. After lunch we went to the plaza above. Peering down past the curve of the waterfall we could see, inside the restaurant, the faces of tourists pressed against the glass, staring up just as we had done.

Dad gave us two dollars each and said, "Now, you can't miss this fountain. We'll meet back here in exactly two hours. Your mother and I will be looking at the Matisse exhibit. Be polite, cross with the lights, keep out of trouble, and you, Shannon, stay with Rianne."

"Don't worry, Dad," I said. "We're going to see the elephant and the dinosaur bones."

And we were, too. But first, as soon as Mom and Dad vanished into the National Gallery's revolving door, I dragged Shannon across the street. Abe had long since stalked off toward the Air and Space Museum.

I had noticed the souvenir and postcard shop while we were looking at the waterfall. We stood on the sidewalk and peered into the dingy window. The posters of the president and the first lady were faded by the sun and weighted down with plastic replicas of the Jefferson Memorial. Colorful signs beside the door said, Se Habla Español and Travelers Checks Cashed and The D.C. Lottery: You Gotta Play to Win. A big air-conditioning unit hummed over the door and dripped water on everyone who went in or out.

When I opened the door, a blast of ice-cold air roared onto my face. Shannon said, "Ooh, look! They sell stickers!" While she looked over the rack to see if there were any she didn't already have, I went up to the cashier.

She was a plump black woman, with her graying hair frizzed out behind a shiny green hair band. She popped her gum and said, "Can I help you, honey?"

"I'd like to buy a lottery ticket," I said.

She looked me up and down with sharp black eyes. "You can't buy one, honey. No one under eighteen's supposed to play."

I could have insisted I was eight years older than I really was. A complete idiot might even have believed me. But this cashier looked very sharp. Without having to think about it I said, "Oh, please! Let me buy one! I'm here for the summer from the Philippines, and I want to show a lottery ticket to my American Government class!"

The cashier heaved a huge sigh. "Shoot. Well, don't nobody win, anyway." She took my dollar, and poised a hand over the console beside her. "You want Daily Double, Lucky Number, or Lucky Lotto?"

I didn't know, and didn't dare to ask. "Lucky Lotto," I said at random.

"You can choose twelve numbers yourself, or let the machine do it."

"I don't care which numbers I get," I said quickly.

The machine clucked and spat out a slip of thin paper with twelve numbers on it. "Here you are, honey. You get two sets of six, see? The winning number will be on TV and in the paper."

Weak with relief, I collected Shannon and left. As we waited to cross the street with the light Shannon said, "You're such a good liar, Rianne."

Her tone held nothing but admiration. For the first time I thought about what a dreadful example I was setting. Suppose my sister grew up to be a psychopath, an ax murderer, because she looked up to me? Guiltily I said, "There's nothing good about it! I just had to get it done, that's all."

I salved my conscience by taking Shannon through the entire dinosaur hall in the Museum of Natural History. It was a popular exhibit, full of little boys in stegosaurus T-shirts. Then we went upstairs and stared at the Hope Diamond and all the other enormous jewels in the mineral collection. Dazzled by their glory, we had to run to meet Mom and Dad on time.

When we got home I examined the ticket more carefully. It looked a lot like an ordinary cash register receipt, except for the words "Lucky Lotto" printed on top. The twelve numbers were printed in two rows of six, just as the cashier had said. This is what they were:

11 13 19 21 23 29
02 03 07 09 16 36

"How did the machine decide on these particular numbers?" Shannon wanted to know.

"The computer chooses them randomly," I said.

"Oh!" She sounded disappointed. "I thought they chose them for you specially—like horoscopes."

I rolled my eyes. "Horoscopes," I echoed. "Now there's random choice for you."

❧5❧

I tried to forget about the lottery until the drawing. But I couldn't help reading the twelve numbers over and over again, until I finally memorized them. The following Wednesday I made sure I got the job of going to the curb to fetch the *Washington Post* from the box.

The lottery results have their own little space in the Metro section. I flipped through to it while Abe grabbed the comics section and Mom slid out the editorial page to look at the political cartoon. And sure enough! Under Lucky Lotto the six winning numbers were listed. They were: 11 13 19 21 23 29.

For about ten minutes I hugged the secret to myself. To know something that nobody else does is the most marvelous feeling. A glass of orange juice and an English muffin steadied me. Of course, to cash in the ticket would be impossible—for me. I was too young, and looked it. Anyway, Shannon could never keep such an exciting secret.

In her own style, Mom was busy making more orange juice. That is, she read the folded paper she held in one hand, while with the other she held the opened can of frozen juice upside down over the pitcher. "Mom," I said, "can I tell you something?"

"Of course, dear," she said, looking up and blinking shortsightedly at me through her glasses. I inherit my own nearsightedness from her. "Are your library books overdue again?"

"No—" I waited until the chunk of frozen juice slid out to plop into the pitcher. "You remember we went downtown last weekend?"

"Yes, darling." Mom began to measure water into the pitcher with the empty can.

"I bought a D.C. lottery ticket with one of the dollars Dad gave me."

"That was silly of you, Rianne," Mom said absently, glancing at her paper again. "You know the odds are millions to one against you. It's throwing money away."

I gulped. "But Mom, I think I won." The chopstick Mom uses to mix juice stirred slower and slower inside the pitcher. "They print the winning number here in the *Post*." I held out the Metro section.

Mom put down the chopstick and editorial, and took the section I gave her. "Do you still have your ticket?"

"Yes." I ran upstairs to fetch it, pausing only to stick my head into Shannon's room and hiss, "Hey, sleepy! We won!" She didn't even roll over!

When I gave the ticket to Mom she looked at it carefully, comparing the numbers printed on it to the ones in the paper. "Do you know what the jackpot is?" Mom asked faintly.

It had never occurred to me to ask. The paper didn't

say anything about it. "No," I admitted. "But I guess it must be something."

"I think we'd better lay this ticket away safely until your father gets up," Mom said in a limp voice. Dad had worked late yesterday, and was sleeping in.

Everyone was up by lunchtime. The meal turned into a sort of family council. Dad, when he recovered from the shock, agreed to turn in the ticket and deposit the check. "What are you going to buy with it, Rianne?" Abe asked eagerly. "How about a motorcycle?"

I didn't bother to answer this, since I was sure Mom or Dad would have something to say about it. "I think it would be very unwise money management to spend it all, however much it amounts to," Mom said quickly.

Dad agreed. "A windfall like this should be laid away for your college fund."

"But we're not going to save it all, Dad—are we?" Abe was appalled.

"No," Dad said uncertainly.

"I think a *little* indulgence isn't unreasonable," Mom said.

"Great!" Shannon put down her hot dog, glowing with excitement. "Let's go to Disney World!"

Abe made a disgusted noise in his throat, and Dad smiled. "That might be too much, pumpkin," he said.

"I think Rianne should have a say," Abe put it. "She bought the ticket."

"Although I wish you wouldn't do it again, Ree," Mom said. "You've used up your beginner's luck, I'm sure."

As a matter of fact, I wasn't. But I obediently agreed, "I won't, Mom. Even the lady who sells them said it's a game for suckers. What do you think about buying a pet?"

We had had a boxer in Greece, but big dogs don't do well in the tropics, and Matso died in Manila. It hadn't been worth getting another animal, since we knew Dad would be reassigned. And Mom is always lukewarm about pets, I guess because she knows who winds up feeding them! But now Dad said what he always says when the subject comes up. "A pet would be good for you kids. Teach you responsibility."

"Remember, now!" Mom said. "Feeding, cleaning, and grooming are chores, too!"

"Oh, let's get a pony!" Shannon cried.

From that point the discussion became hot and heavy. Matso had been especially Abe's dog, and he wanted a puppy, a boxer again, if possible. Mom suggested goldfish, guinea pigs, and white mice, all without any takers. I wanted a cat. And Shannon's heart was instantly set on a pony, a palomino one. When Abe hooted at this she shouted, "I never get to choose ANYTHING, just because I'm the youngest!"

"Now, let me inject some rational analysis into this discussion," Dad interrupted. "We don't have a very big yard, Shannon. And it isn't fenced. Have you thought about where a pony would live?"

"Could we build it a shed?" Shannon said, without much hope. "And maybe it could eat tree leaves? We could name it Goldie."

"I don't think that's possible, darling," Mom soothed her. "Besides, there are zoning laws about such big animals."

"But not about dogs," Abe said. "And I would walk the dog, every day."

"We still don't have a fenced yard," Dad repeated. "What will happen to the dog while you're at school?"

"Mom could keep him in the house, to guard against burglars."

Dad looked at Mom, who shook her head at the idea. "I think Abe was right," she said. "Rianne bought the ticket, and she should get a choice."

"Hurray, a kitty!" I cried.

"But Abe and Shannon must help choose it," Mom added. "And all of you must help take care of it."

"Oh, well, a cat is okay, I guess," Abe conceded.

"Let's pick a kitten, Ree," Shannon begged. "A fluffy white one."

On Thursday Dad went to work, promising to redeem the ticket over his lunch hour. He phoned in the afternoon to tell us what happened. The Lucky Lotto jackpot came to $1,000—not enough to take a family of five to Disney World, as even Shannon had to admit. Instead, Mom drove us all to the county animal shelter. We had never been to such a place before. It's a very American idea. In a lot of foreign countries there are so many problems feeding and housing people, no one worries much about animals.

We felt very grown up when Mom made Abe and me promise beforehand not to tell Shannon that most of the animals in the shelter are killed if no one adopts them. "No fear, Mom!" Abe said. "I don't want two zillion cats and dogs living here either."

"Yeah, she would make us adopt them all, to save them from the grave," I said.

The shelter was a long, gray building. Inside, the dogs were each in their own pen, long, echoing rows of them like a jail. It was kind of depressing when they all wagged their tails and jumped against the doors and barked a welcome at us. Abe was more resigned about getting a cat when he didn't see any boxers there. Shannon bounced like a pinball from one cage to another, calling, "Look at this one, Mom! Can we take him? Ooh, here's a collie. Why can't we have him, we could name him Lassie!"

Pretending not to hear, Mom said. "Oh, look, children, here's the cutest little calico kitten!" So Shannon was distracted into the cat room. The cages were smaller here, and stacked up in tiers around the walls. I looked at every cat carefully. There were little kittens and full-grown cats. Some were just cat cats, tabby or gray or orange. But there were some fancy breeds too. Mom took a paperback edition of *Sir Gawain and the Green Knight* out of her purse and began to read. She applied to enter a masters degree program in medieval literature last week. She knew it would take us hours to make a decision.

Abe stuck his finger into a cage holding a Russian Blue. It was a beautiful cat, with plushy, deep blue-gray fur, and it looked at Abe's finger out of aristocratic golden eyes. "What we need is a classy cat," he said, reaching to pet it.

"Just don't choose a tempery one," Mom said without looking up.

A man in an overall with a badge came by and said, "Shall I take him out for you?"

"Oh, can we hold him?" Shannon cried.

44

But before he could unlock the door the cat lunged across the cage and stuck his claws hard into Abe's finger. "Ow!" he yelled, and whipped his finger out.

"Maybe not that one," I said to the attendant. "How about this white one?"

In the end we took out and held almost every cat there. Some of them we took out twice. It was hard to decide, even after weeding out any mean ones. But finally after a lot of spirited discussion we agreed on a young white and orange cat. She purred when any of us held her, a very persuasive talent. Even Abe was convinced, when she rolled over in his arms and looking adoringly up into his face with big green eyes. Mom signed some papers and paid an adoption fee, and she was ours.

We spent the ride home arguing about her name. "I want her to be Jane," I said. "After Jane Eyre."

"She doesn't look like Jane Eyre," Shannon said, even though she hasn't read the book.

"Oh, yes she does," I said, from the front seat. "She has green eyes. And also, we rescued her when she was going to die."

Abe, who was sitting just behind me, gave my hair a painful jerk. "Why was she going to die?" Shannon wanted to know. "The cat, not Jane in the book."

"I mean, when she didn't have any friends and was in trouble," I gabbled hastily.

"I think Jane is a perfect name," Abe said almost as quickly. "Here, Jane, come on out and be named."

"Now Abe, leave that cat in its box," Mom warned. "I don't want her careening around in this car while I'm driving."

With a fearful wail Jane leaped out like a jack-in-the-box on its spring. In the safety of the cardboard box she had traveled quietly enough, but now the sight of the trees flicking past and the road sliding by terrified her. "Yow, she clawed me!" Abe yelled.

"I'll grab her," Shannon said.

Mom turned to look but had to turn back quickly before the car ran off the narrow road. "Get that animal back into the box!" she snapped. "And whatever you do, don't let it climb into the front seat, or we'll have an accident."

Shannon pounced and grabbed Jane by the scruff. The cat screamed like a soul in torment, wriggling violently. Quickly Abe lifted the box up. I knelt backward on the front seat and lifted the flaps. As soon as Shannon dropped her in Jane hooked a foot on the box rim. But I slammed the flaps down anyway. It took us the rest of the drive to unhook her paw, claw by claw, from the edge of the box. By the time we were done we all had scratched fingers. Our only consolation was that Shannon's attention had been quite drawn off from questions about Jane's name.

6

In spite of this rocky beginning Jane settled down well enough. We bought her a green leather collar and a tag with her name and address on it. Mom wouldn't let her sleep indoors, but Jane could come inside if we kept an eye on her. She spent her nights in the garage, until we were sure she knew this was her house. In the daytime she chased butterflies and took catnaps on the deck, where we also put her cat food and water. There was much less work than when we had Matso, no walks on a leash or grooming mats out of fur. Mom even went so far as to say, "Cats are easier pets than goldfish."

It was through Jane that we met the Impossumble again. June was almost over, and the weather turned hot and muggy. The house was cooled with air conditioning, but I liked the outdoors because it reminded me of Manila. In the evening after the dishwasher was loaded I liked to sit on the deck. A month ago I wouldn't have believed it, but it really isn't much work clearing dishes away.

Jane climbed into my lap and purred. A rhythmic, shrill noise of insects filled the twilight air. Far away

47

through the trees I could just see the lights of other houses. Probably in wintertime they would be plain enough to see, but now the deck was totally private, armored in leaves. Behind me the door slid back. Abe drew up a chair and said, "I picked up a flea collar for Jane." Mom had bought new deck chairs so more than one of us could sit. Jane hardly even opened an eye as Abe buckled the collar on. "Too fat and sassy," he commented, as he snipped off the excess length.

It was completely dark now, and the moon was rising above the trees. It looked like a piece of lemon peel, not like green cheese at all. Then very quietly Abe jogged my elbow. "Ree, look!" he muttered. "At the cat's dish. Gently!"

Slowly I looked over my shoulder. A familiar opossum form was sitting on the top step, calm as you please, and munching cat food from Jane's dish. I grinned in the darkness, looking forward to Abe's astonishment. "Hello, Impossumble—is that you?"

"Quiet, Ree, you'll scare it!" Abe hushed me.

But the Impossumble sat up on her fat haunches and said, "Is that *boy* safe? What about the animal?"

"Who, Jane?" I tickled the cat's chin. "She's too lazy to chase visitors. And Abe is my brother."

"It *talks!*" Abe yelped.

"Not too loud," I warned him in my turn.

"I don't like cats," the Impossumble grumbled.

"You seem to like their food."

"Is that what this stuff is?" The Impossumble nosed another pellet up from the bowl and crunched it. "Dreadful. If cats have to live on this I can see why they chase mice." She reminded me of Dad, wolfing

48

down corn chips while explaining to us that they were full of salt and saturated fats that would clog your arteries and turn you heart into a limp blob of lard.

"I hope you got those apples we brought you," I said.

"I found them, but while I was carrying one home a squirrel stole the rest." The Impossumble's complaining voice squeaked like a rusty iron gate. "You should have delivered them to my den. But I suppose I can't blame you, since I'm not going to tell you where it is."

"Please don't, if it would make you in any way uneasy," I said politely, imitating the civilized tone I had heard Mom use at embassy Christmas parties. Apparently being a nocturnal animal had nothing to do with it. It was quite dark now, and she must be well rested, but the Impossumble was crabby as ever.

Under this courtesy the Impossumble unbent a little. "I was glad to get my coverlet back," she said. "Thanks."

"You're very welcome," I said, as warmly as I could. "I'm glad to know you got it all right, it was on my mind."

"I suppose all this soft soap means you want another bit of luck," the Impossumble growled.

"No, it doesn't," I said indignantly. "I wasn't thinking about that at all. You aren't polite to people, or animals either, just to worm favors out of them. Right, Abe?"

I kicked him lightly on the ankle, and Abe blurted, "That's right. It's what Mom always says."

The Impossumble was interested. "Then what good is it?" she asked.

I had never thought about it before. "Well—courtesy is, um—"

"The oil that greases the wheels of society," Abe suggested.

I didn't have to look at the Impossumble to see that she never greased engines. "It's doing to other folks what you would like done to yourself," I said, vaguely remembering some Sunday school lesson. "If I were you, I would have wanted my coverlet back. It was a nice one. So it was polite to return it."

"That's an incredible way to manage," the Impossumble said. "Does this mean I have to be polite, too?"

"Only if you want to."

No one said anything for a bit. The Impossumble ate another few bites of cat food, and then hunched herself irritably. "Oh well! You could use another bit of luck."

"No, we're doing fine," I said, in all honesty.

"Yes, you do," the Impossumble said grumpily, turning away. "You really need it now."

Abe was using a finger to make little circles at the side of his head. I frowned at him and called, "If you like, I could bring out another apple."

The Impossumble hesitated, but then went on down the steps into the backyard. "No, I refuse to become a pet!" And she vanished into the night.

"Whew!" Abe whistled and leaned back in his chair. "A talking, magical animal! How did you find it?"

"*She* is an opossum," I said, and told him how we had met. "The Impossumble told us to buy the lottery ticket," I concluded.

50

"She did? Holy cow!" Abe planted both feet on the deck and leaned forward to look at me. "Do you realize what we could do with this, Rianne?"

"We're not going to do anything to the Impossumble," I said. "Remember Bobby Canfield."

"You're too secretive about things, Ree," Abe said, in a really aggravating older-brother way. "You should have consulted me sooner. Of course I don't mean *catching* her. But you could give her more apples, make her an opossum house for the winter—oh, lots of things. Really cultivate her, you know?"

"Except that she wouldn't accept an apple tonight."

"Think about how useful she could be," he went on, without bothering to answer me. "Say, in Dad's line of work. The U.S. government really needs an extra push of luck every now and then."

I could see why the Impossumble was nervous about people. "I think the government gets along okay on its own," I argued. "It's like tennis. Would it be as much fun to win tennis matches if you knew that the Impossumble had weighted things in your favor?"

"Now, tennis is a very good example," Abe said. "Do you realize how often luck is a factor, a major factor, in a tournament? The wind, the way the ball bounces—"

It was hopeless. What a dummy I was to bring up tennis! Abe talked for another twenty minutes about notable games played by Ivan Lendl or Bjorn Borg. I sat patiently encouraging him, whenever he flagged, with expressions of interest. I was bored rigid, but I thought the less he talked about the Impossumble, the better.

51

The following Thursday was the Fourth of July. We all agreed with Mom when she proposed driving downtown to see the fireworks. We had an early dinner and drove down in plenty of time to get a good seat on the grass near the Lincoln Memorial.

While Mom and Dad lay on the picnic blanket we kids climbed up the steps to the monument. A blue and purple evening, clear as glass, arched over us and made the marble columns look very white. In the echoing big chamber we instinctively dropped our voices to whispers. The enormous, pale statue of Lincoln seated on his chair seemed to look out over the mall with calm interest.

When we got back to the blanket Shannon said, "He doesn't look anything like our Abe. How did Grandpa come to name him that?"

Dad and I guffawed. Abe scowled at Shannon, while Mom said, "Abe is named after Grandpa's father, dear—your great-grandfather Abraham Prosper Makenside. But I believe *he* really was named after Abraham Lincoln. He was a Civil War baby." Mom always knows things like that; so much so that none of us will play Trivial Pursuit with her anymore.

"You don't have to look like someone to be named after them," I chortled. "Oh, ho, ho! But what Abe would look like, with chin whiskers!" I lay on the blanket and kicked my heels up with laughter.

"At least I'm named after someone real," Abe growled. "Not like Marianne."

I sat up as if he had stuck a pin in me. My full name is hateful, like someone in a soppy romance novel, and I never use it. Even Rianne is too close. When I get the nerve I'm going to change my name to Riannon, it's much prettier. If only Mom hadn't been taking a course in Jane Austen before I was born! "Don't you start that!" I yelled.

Abe and Shannon began capering around like morons, chanting, "MAR-ianne, MAR-ianne!"

But Mom put a stop to it. "Sit down and be quiet," she commanded. "I'm going to open the doughnuts."

Dad sat up to root around in the picnic basket. There were doughnuts, and oranges, and a plastic jug of lemonade, too. By the time we ate everything it was dark enough for the fireworks to start.

They were beautiful, much finer than any we had seen before. The sight of the tall spire of the Washington Monument, silhouetted by fountains of red and blue sparks, made us all feel patriotic and proud. There were big, round blossoms of color, like chrysanthemums of light, and curlicue fireworks that corkscrewed down the sky.

As we crawled along in the colossal traffic jam leaving town I said, "I'm glad we're staying in the States a few years."

"Well, there's a change!" Mom said cheerfully. "I thought you would be homesick for Manila forever."

Dad said, "Now we're over the bridge I'm going to get off the highway and use the local roads. Nothing can be as bad as this."

The station wagon popped and groaned as Dad gunned the engine. We nipped out the Vienna exit and onto Nutley Street. From somewhere ahead came the sound of many horns honking.

"Someone's having a happy Fourth," Abe said.

Then I saw the headlights. The street was divided by an island, but they were on *our* side! With incredible speed they grew bigger and brighter. Dad slammed on his brakes and leaned on the horn. "Donald!" Mom cried to Dad. "He's still coming!" The lights glared horribly into our eyes, like searchlights.

Dad stamped on the gas so suddenly we were jerked back in our seats. He spun the wheel hard to the right as the dreadful lights zoomed down on us. With a tremendous splintering crash something slapped the tail of our car. The impact threw us all to one side against our seat belts. The car nearly rolled right over. The world seemed to whirl around very fast. Our car screeched on two wheels, skidding into a stand of young trees at the side of the road.

Then for a moment everything was very still. From a long way away came the sound of jabbering voices and wailing sirens. In a perfectly calm voice Dad said, "Is everyone all right? Get out of the car if you can. I smell gasoline."

I found myself standing some way away in the grass, but I couldn't remember unbuckling my seat belt or opening the door. Abe limped up, unabashedly clutching Mom's hand. Mom's face was gray. Dad followed, carrying Shannon. Two or three police cars were pulling up, blinking their red roof lights. "Sit down, Irene," Dad said to Mom.

"I'm just shaken up," Mom said. She straightened her glasses and sat down heavily on the shaggy grass. We sat, too, huddling as close as we could. Some policemen came to talk to Dad. Others helped some-

one out of the other car. In the further lane rubber-
neckers slowed down to gawk at us. Traffic began to
back up on our side, and also down the exit ramp and
into the highway. With a great screaming of sirens
two ambulances drove up.

A policeman came and squatted down by us. "How
do you feel, ma'am? Anyone hurt?"

"No, we've been very lucky," Mom said, more
steadily now. "What about the other driver?"

"Drunk as a skunk, ma'am," the policeman said,
shaking his head. "Two empty sixpacks in the back
seat."

"I'm hurt," Abe suddenly burst out. "The seat belt cut into my hip."

"Probably saved your life." The cop stood up. "It might be better for you all to get checked over right away by a doctor. You're a real lucky bunch of folks."

"Oh, we are!" I agreed fervently.

It wasn't nearly as much fun as I would have thought, to ride in an ambulance. For one thing, the siren yelled continuously right above us, and made my head ache. Since none of us needed to lie down on the stretchers we all sat up in the back of one ambulance. A sort of reaction set in. After being as quiet as a mouse all this time Shannon suddenly burst into loud sobs. "I don't want us to die, Mommy!" she wailed, hugging Mom's neck.

"Nobody does, dear," Mom said, hugging her back.

Hysterical tears choked my throat too, and Abe said, "Shannon's seat belt was stuck. Dad cut it with his pocketknife."

"I'm going to carry it from now on," Dad promised, squeezing my hand. "To remind me how important my family's safety is."

When we got to the hospital we had to wait for hours. No one minded, though, after Mom pointed out that they would hurry to treat you if you were hurt badly enough. The doctors found a graze on Abe's hip where his seat belt had dug into his jeans. Mom had a bruise on her elbow, and I had one on my knee. That was all. By the time we got home, in a taxi, it was almost three in the morning.

7

It took us several days to stop jittering. When Mom and Dad went out to buy a new car none of us insisted on tagging along. Under normal circumstances we all three would have squeezed into the back of Dad's old sports car. And at the car dealers we would have helped to choose a car by slamming the doors on showroom models, and fiddling with their electric windows.

"It'll be a new experience for me, to shop for a vehicle in a civilized manner," Dad tried to cheer us up. "I'll just have to bear up under the strain."

After they drove off, Shannon and I continued listlessly watching a rerun of "The Flintstones." Then Abe stood up and switched it off. "Hey!" Shannon protested.

"This is garbage," Abe said impatiently. "We have something more important to do than turn into couch potatoes."

My brain felt like it was padded in Styrofoam. "Yeah? Like what?"

"We have to bring some apples down into the woods for that opossum."

57

I didn't feel this was worth answering. Shannon said, "Oh, Abe, I couldn't!"

"Why not?"

Shannon's mouth began to quiver. "I want that Impossumble to go away. I'm scared of her. We could have been killed, you know!"

"Of course I know, runt!" Abe said. "She told Rianne we'd get some luck, and we did—in spades! We were *incredibly* lucky to walk away from that crash." He turned to me "You've got to feel *some* gratitude, Ree."

"I guess," I said.

"Well then, let's express it! That's only manners, right? Like you said the other day."

"Oh, all right," I groaned, getting up. "Anything for a little peace."

"But you have to hold my hand," Shannon said. Abe tried to tell her only babies did that, but she insisted. We threaded our way into the woods out back, me leading the way with the apples in a paper bag.

It was a blazing hot July day. The sky was blurred with a milky haze that let the sunshine scorch through but held the heat in like a lid. A weak, humid breeze trailed through the tips of the leaves, as if it were too limp and hot to do more. Bits of last year's leaves got into my sneakers, and Shannon scratched her ankle on a thorn.

In just these few weeks the underbrush had grown amazingly. We couldn't walk between the trees anymore. Instead, we had to force our way through leaves and stubborn vines, like swimmers plowing their way through ocean surf. The very first settlers in Virginia must have been supermen, to have done anything with these woods. To clear a few acres and plant crops would break my back for sure. I couldn't find the fallen tree we had used before. I couldn't even be sure we were near it. So it was a great relief when, in the crotch of a tree, I saw a pointed pink snout poke out.

"You sound like lame cows, lumbering along like that," the Impossumble greeted us. "I suppose you realize you've scared off every edible bug for a mile around."

"Well, we brought you some apples, so you've got nothing to beef about," Abe retorted, probably more crossly than he had meant.

"We were very grateful for the luck," I said. "And we wanted to thank you. Would you like to carry them to your hole while we wait? Then no one will steal them."

I balanced an apple on a lower branch, and the Impossumble surveyed it warily. Then she slipped down and picked it up in her mouth. Even with this awkward burden she made scarcely a rustle as she vanished into the undergrowth. There was nowhere for us to sit while we waited. Shannon flopped down onto the ground but got up again quickly because it was wet. Abe leaned against a scrub oak and scratched his mosquito bites. I wiped the sweat from my glasses with the hem of my T-shirt.

"Okay," said the Impossumble's rusty little voice. "Hand up another one." She took it and slipped off.

"You and your big ideas," Abe carped in a whisper. "This is a bore. And these bugs are eating me alive."

"It was *your* idea," I retorted. "Your problem is you have no patience or tact."

"Well, don't just hand over the next one! Hang on to it a while, so we can keep her talking!"

So when the Impossumble reappeared on her tree branch I held the paper bag shut and said to Abe, "Okay, talk—now's your big chance!"

Abe shot me an aggravated glance, and licked his lips. "Uh, does this hot weather bother you?"

"No," the Impossumble said briefly. She looked rather irritated at being spoken to. "This is my natural habitat."

"Oh, good topic," I applauded Abe. "The weather! Now bring up the Mets or the Orioles, why don't you."

"There's an oriole's nest down by the stream," the Impossumble said suspiciously. "What's a Met? Is it good to eat?"

The whole session would have disintegrated into wrangling, except for Shannon. She looked up at the Impossumble and said, "I want to know why we had an accident at all. That's not what I call lucky."

Abe slapped his forehead in frustration. The Impossumble eyed the last apple in my hand and said, "You don't know anything about it. The fact is, you were all up for some broken bones, at least. But human beings don't value their health at all, what with their cigarettes and beer and so on."

"Yes, we do," Shannon said very seriously. "I brush my teeth every night. That shows I know they're important."

"Your *teeth!* I'm amazed you're still alive!" The

60

Impossumble stared down into Shannon's upturned face as if she were insane. Of course, animals never brush, or floss either. Then she scowled at me. "Are you going to eat that apple yourself, or what?"

"Sorry!" I set it on the lower branch and once more the Impossumble popped down to get it.

Abe hastily spoke up. "So we've had wealth and health. What else is there? Happiness?"

The Impossumble kept a paw on the apple as she said, "Sure, if you like."

"Please don't bother if it's an effort for you," I said. "I remember a book about a Psammead who hated to do magic."

But as she bit into her apple the Impossumble showed not a speck of interest in other magical animals. "Thanks," she mumbled, and crept off.

We set off again back up the hill. "See?" Abe said. "If it hadn't been for me we wouldn't have gotten another dab of good luck!"

"I still think it's pushy," I said. "Like when Shannon climbs into Grandma's lap and says, 'Gimme a present.' "

"I haven't done that since I was a baby," Shannon objected, scowling like a very small thundercloud.

"Good manners can't be as important as this," Abe maintained. "We have to get while the getting is good." Before we could argue anymore about it there came a crashing, rustly noise from the other side of the valley.

"I hope that isn't a bear," I said.

"Oh, I want to see a bear!" Shannon exclaimed.

"What a moronic wish," Abe began. But suddenly

the branches were pushed aside by a big man. He wore jeans, work boots, and thick work gloves. "Hi, kids," he said casually.

"What are you doing here?" Abe asked, and I could tell he was thinking about the Impossumble.

"Surveying," the man said, and we saw he was carrying a collapsible tripod under his arm.

"The cluster houses," I remembered.

"Yep. You haven't seen an orange stake around here, have you? It would be stuck in the ground, to mark the property line."

"No," Abe said.

"You'll have to be Daniel Boone to find anything in this jungle," I added.

We left him scuffling around in the underbrush, and went home for some lemonade.

Mom and Dad eventually decided on a dark green Subaru station wagon. "Now if it had been a white Jaguar convertible, that might have been our luck," Abe commented the evening they brought it home, but of course he's getting his driver's license next year. This car was so *normal* that as we cleared away the dinner dishes we agreed it couldn't possibly be "happiness."

"And what does happiness mean, anyway?" I asked, picking up the silverware. "What makes you happy might not make, say, Shannon happy."

"No, a Jaguar wouldn't make me happy at all," Shannon said. "A pony—that's what happiness is."

"Yick," Abe said. He held the handful of forks and knives under the tap for a few seconds, and then dropped them into the dishwasher.

"Let me by for a second, son," Dad said. He turned the water to run cold and filled his glass. "What are you kids chattering so seriously about?"

"Happiness," I said quickly, before Shannon could blurt out anything. "If you could have whatever you wanted, Daddy, what would make you happiest?"

Dad fished some ice cubes out of the bin in the freezer and dropped them into his glass. "Ice cream," he said, rolling his blue eyes around in the way that always makes Shannon laugh. "Maple walnut, on a sugar cone, with chocolate sprinkles. Let's go out and get some!"

"Yes, let's!" Shannon whooped.

"Oh, Dad, you're not being serious," I said, but he was already calling to Mom to put on her shoes and get her purse.

8

For a few days we buzzed around in a fever of anticipation, waiting for a bonanza. There was always a crazy dash for the mailbox when the postman came, in case something exciting came in a letter. Abe read the political columns in the *Post* carefully, in case Dad became appointed Secretary of State or something. And I made a big effort, hanging around the swimming pool hoping to meet some friends. All I got was water in my ears. But nothing happened, and after a while we sort of relaxed.

We had started to go to church again. Ever since he became a real teenager Abe has dragged his heels about it. So we thought it was tremendously funny when he met a girl there, toward the end of July. She was a little, brown-haired girl like a sparrow, named Amber Doherty. Shannon and I found out her name by looking in the church picture directory, because Abe refused to say one word about her. But all of a sudden he was really gung ho about the teen roller-skating expedition, and the pickup volleyball game on Wednesday nights.

"So you're switching to volleyball?" I asked him,

leaning against the bathroom door and making my eyes very innocent and wide. "Isn't Boris Becker your ideal any more?"

Abe was combing his hair for the eighth time. "Shut up, Ree," he said very fiercely. He inspected his reflection narrowly, and then began combing again.

Shannon leaned on the other door post, and stuck her tongue out in a thoughtful way at her reflection in the big bathroom mirror. "You aren't as big a star in volleyball," she said. "You're only one member of a team. I think singles in tennis is better, if you want to be in American Express commercials."

"But some people do prefer volleyball, regardless," I said, grinning. "Some Amber-gers."

"Get out!" Abe exploded, and banged the door on us. He locked it, too.

"Hark!" Shannon said rather loudly to me, and cupped a hand to her ear. "Do I hear the whoosh of hair mousse?"

"He might *think* he's hidden the can," I said, with my mouth close to the door. "But I saw the cardboard sleeve in the trash can!" We leaned against the wall and giggled until the tears ran down our faces.

Abe jerked the door open and hissed, "You snoopy brats!" He barreled down the steps and out the door.

We ran to Shannon's room and hung out the window. As Abe pumped his bike up the driveway on his way to church I yelled, "Yep, he's got mousse!" Then we rolled on the bed, laughing.

When I went downstairs for a drink Mom had all her books spread out on the dining room table. She was planning her master's thesis, even though she hadn't been accepted into the program yet. I got a lemonade and sat down. I turned the nearest book around so I could read the title. It was *The Romance of the Rose.*

"Be careful with your drink, Rianne," Mom said, turning a page. "I don't want my books to get sticky."

"What's this one about, Mom?"

"Oh, it's an allegorical love story." I didn't know what allegorical was, but didn't want to say so. For a while we sat quietly, Mom using her pink highlighter on a passage or two in her book, and me sipping carefully at my lemonade. Then without looking up Mom said, "I wish you wouldn't tease Abe so much, Ree."

"Who, me?" I said guiltily.

Mom closed the book on the highlighter, to mark her place. "If he's been able to make friends and participate in activities, that's good," she said.

I hung my head. "I guess I'm a little jealous, Mom," I said sadly. "I'm lonesome and bored too, and there's nobody for me to hang around with."

"It's hard for you now, dear," Mom said. "When school starts you'll meet lots of kids your own age."

All of a sudden depression hit me, like a landslide of dark, heavy mud. "Why is it so easy for Abe? He can just slide right into the swing of things. Is there something wrong with me?"

"Well, Abe is older than you," Mom said. "And your personalities are different. You've always been quieter and more reserved."

"Secretive," I said bitterly.

"You're not very communicative, no," Mom agreed. "But that's just the way you are."

I flipped through *The Romance of the Rose* to see if there were any pictures. There weren't. "Do you think the Amber girl makes Abe happy?" I asked.

Mom smiled. "I'm sure he wouldn't describe it that way. And he doesn't always act happy. But yes—in spite of everything, I think Abe is enjoying himself a lot. It's one of the big watersheds when you become a teenager, you know—getting interested in the other sex." She opened her book again. "So have a little sympathy, okay?"

"I guess," I said. But I still felt depressed. Usually I have a stable, self-sufficient kind of temperament. When I didn't feel better the next morning, I decided to do something. If Abe could do it, so could I. I resolved to go somewhere that day and strike up a conversation with somebody my own age.

I wavered for a while between the library and the shopping center. You can't talk very well in libraries. On the other hand, spending time in the shopping center means spending money sooner or later. Our allowances are pathetically tiny. That's another reason why I needed to make some friends—so that I could prove to Mom and Dad that I'm drastically under-funded!

In the end, I bicycled to the library. The weather was hot and sticky, with the sun shining like a red-hot penny in the sky. The library's air conditioning felt good. The Reston library is a classy, modern building, with lots more books than the American School's library in Manila. I went through the whole building. There were babies and kids rampaging through the children's room, and old men very slowly reading the *New York Times* and the *Wall Street Journal* near the newspaper racks.

The only possible prospect from my point of view was a boy poring over a recent issue of *Rolling Stone* in the magazine room. He looked about thirteen, with sunburn and freckles on his nose. I have a lot of nerve, but not enough to scrape up an acquaintance with a *boy!* The only thing I could think of to do was to sit in a nearby armchair and flick through *Seventeen.* Of course, this got me exactly nowhere. After about ten minutes a woman came by with an armload of books and said, "I'm ready, Brett, what about you?" And he got up and left with her. I was so disgusted I didn't finish my magazine. Obviously, the bit of luck wasn't going to be mine!

The next day Shannon was first to the mailbox after the postman drove by. I met her at the door. "Give me the magazines," I said.

She did, leafing through the circulars and announcements of summer sales. "Oh, look, Ree!"

There was a long, thick envelope from Georgetown University, addressed to Mom. "Hurry!" I said. "Let's take it to her!"

Mom was boning a leg of lamb, but she dropped her knife the moment we shouted the news. She tore open the envelope while Shannon and I jittered with excitement and yelled comments like, "Oh, don't wait to wipe your hands, Mom! What's a little lamb juice!" and "It must be good news, Mom, the letter's so fat!"

"They've accepted me!" she cried. "I can start in September!"

We hugged her, shouting, "Congratulations, Mom!"

That was a happy time. Mom's face glowed with joy. Dad took her out to dinner at Auberge Chez François, a fancy French restaurant, to celebrate.

While they were out we kids baked a cake in her honor. I wanted chocolate while Abe insisted on white angel food. We compromised on marble fudge, from a mix, of course. The can of red squirt-on frosting ran out before we put on as many curlicues and flowers as we wanted. Only then did someone notice that we had written "Congradulations" with a *d* and not a *t*. Shannon insisted she could fix it, by sort of swooshing up the misspelled letter with her finger. But we older ones wouldn't let her try. We were sure she would just smear up everything. In spite of this it was a great success. Mom said the cake was tastier than the one at the restaurant. I think what really delighted her was that we cleaned up the kitchen after ourselves—perfectly! You would never know that a cake had been baked in it, except for the smell of chocolate.

Mom began preparations for graduate school right away. She bought a big freezer and had the delivery men set it up in the basement. Then she began cooking—casseroles, bread, vegetable gratins, pie. All of it went into the freezer, to be defrosted again in September or October when no one had time to cook. Abe bought produce at the farmers' market every day. I cut up enough zucchini and tomatoes to fill a bathtub. Shannon hauled so many vats of pot roast or spaghetti sauce down to the freezer that she forgot to worry about Mr. Amontillado. "And then I'm going to can peaches," Mom proposed. We groaned at the idea, even though there's nothing better in February than peaches canned by Mom in August.

While I scalded a million peaches in boiling water and zipped off their thin, fragrant skins I had plenty of time to think. If the Impossumble hadn't told me to, I never would have bought a lottery ticket. But what about Amber Doherty? Would Abe have never met her, if the Impossumble hadn't tipped the scales? Maybe they would have met, and nothing would have happened. They might even have actively disliked each other.

The university acceptance was another puzzle. Mom believed she had got in on her own merits. But had she? What if she were really not qualified at all, and the Impossumble had bamboozled the college, somehow?

There was no point in even mentioning Amber's name to Abe—he'd just glare at me, and press his lips together. It's no wonder people have to write to Ask Beth, and read romance comics, if their own brothers are so closemouthed! But while we shucked corn I did bring up the subject of Mom's master's degree. "Did she get in fair and square?" I asked him.

"Of course." Abe sounded indignant.

"There's no of course about it," I persisted. "If the Impossumble's luck got her in, then she didn't do it herself. And if she would have got in anyway, what did we need the Impossumble for?"

We were sitting on the deck, so that the cornsilk wouldn't make too much of a mess. Mom would trim the cleaned ears to the same length before freezing them. Abe threw down a handful of husks. "Why do you always ask these complicated questions?"

"You're older than I am—why don't you know the answers?"

He picked irritably at the cornsilk stuck between the kernels of his corn. "No one can answer things like that," he said. "And it's unimportant, anyway. The acceptance is only a step. Mom still has to do the *work*. If she doesn't do that, she won't get the degree, and being accepted won't mean a thing."

I could recognize the sense of that; the university was smart enough to choose good students. Abe went on, "I've got different questions. Like, do countries have luck?"

"Huh?"

"Like the Sudan, for instance. There's a basket case—drought, famine, crop failures, political unrest. Or Bangladesh, remember?"

I remembered, from when our plane stopped there once for repairs. It's not a fun country at all. "Yeah, Bangladesh has the short end of the stick, all right. Do you think the Impossumble would do something about it?"

"Of course not; I bet she doesn't even know where Bangladesh is. But what about the U.S.A.?"

"What about it? I think we're pretty lucky, on the whole."

"Sure, in history. But I'm thinking about the future. Suppose there's a nuclear war. Even the Impossumble would notice a nuclear winter, or fallout. That would be bad luck for everybody, including her."

I looked up past the treetops at the slow summer twilight. The sky was a color exactly between blue and purple. Against it the trees looked like black lace. It was hard to imagine bombs falling out of that loveliness. "I wish you hadn't taken American Government last year," I complained. "You make me worry. I bet the Impossumble doesn't know the first thing about atom bombs."

"Well, shouldn't she?"

"What do you want to do, buy her a subscription to the *Post?*"

"At least we could go down and tell her about it."

"What, now?"

"Sure, why not? It's almost dark, she'll be out. And we could give her an ear of corn." Abe stood up, brandishing the last shucked ear like a sword—or a tennis racket.

"Okay, okay." I dumped my corn husks into the trash bag and followed him down the deck steps. "If only I could be sure you weren't going to ask her to improve your backhand."

"Come on," he called, "before it gets too dark."

It was already night under the trees. Ahead of me Abe's T-shirt gleamed slim and white in the darkness. We thrashed down the hill past the tot lot and through the ferns and undergrowth until it was too tangled to pass. "If she doesn't come when we call we'll never find her in all this."

"She must've heard us, like last time. We made enough noise." Abe peered around at the jungly growth. It was dark and close and very moist, like being in the bottom of a swimsuit pocket. "Impossumble!" he yelled softly. "You try, Ree."

"Impossumble!" I called. "We brought you something to eat!" We listened, but the wind stirring in the upper branches masked any animal noise. "Maybe we should just leave it."

"Oh, no—what's the point of a treat if we don't give it to her ourselves?"

"What treat?" The little rusty voice came from right over our heads. "I don't want your bribes. I know that trick."

"He meant that we wanted to be sure you got it," I said quickly. "It's an ear of corn. Have you ever eaten one?"

Abe held it up. The Impossumble leaned down and twitched her white whiskers. She sniffed, "Well, I guess I could taste it. Stick it in the crotch of that branch there."

"Please," Abe added for her in an undertone, but balanced the corn where she wanted it.

The Impossumble waited until he moved back before scuttling down and smelling the corn over. Then she took a tentative nibble. "Go away," she snarled over her shoulder. "I don't like anyone to watch me eat. Too much like the Pet Farm."

"How come you can't be polite?" Abe demanded.

"Wild animals don't have to be," the Impossumble said, crunching into the corn. "But I will say, this is very good."

"We like it, too," I said.

Abe doesn't approve of beating around the bush. "I had some questions about luck," he announced. "Could you tell me how far your ability can reach?"

"You see! I knew it!" With a flip of the paw the Impossumble sent the corn rolling to the ground, where it vanished immediately into the deep litter of dry leaves. "That's just the way it always works—a big present to lull the appetite, and then pry and poke!"

This was so very nearly true that Abe was outraged. "We're so nice to you, you could be a little bit nice to us! I was just asking a question!"

I jogged his elbow and hissed, "Will you be more tactful? Don't just bull your way in!" Then more loudly I said, "We're just making conversation, Impossumble."

In the twilight I could just see her eyes gleam as the Impossumble glared at me. "What's conversation?"

"It's, uh, when friends chat. Talk about things of mutual interest."

"That's right," Abe said, picking up the ball. "That's why I brought up the subject of luck. After all, we don't have that much in common except luck."

"Then I never converse," the Impossumble said, very cross. "I don't have any friends."

"We'll be your friends if you like," I said. "Everybody should have friends."

"Opossums are solitary creatures," the Impossumble grumbled. "There are two of you—why don't *you* converse, and I'll listen and get the hang of it."

Startled, I said, "Uh, okay. Abe, you wanna begin?"

"Thanks a lot. Um, Ree and I were discussing whether countries have luck." He paused, but the Impossumble evidently wasn't going to say whether they did or not. "We wondered, if this country got into trouble or anything, whether you'd interfere."

The Impossumble yawned. "What's a country?"

"Oh, boy. Well, a country is a political entity. Everyone in this country, for instance, is ruled by a bicameral legislature based in Washington, D.C., just down the highway from here. . . ."

74

Abe got real good grades in government class, and he doesn't mind who knows it. Of course, it's more interesting when you don't actually live in the U.S. Then it's more like studying a foreign country. I stood in the muggy dark, with the damp seeping into my sneakers, and groaned. Conversation, huh! Lecture was more like it.

He had just gotten to the differences between the legislative, judicial, and executive branches when a distant yell came from up the hill. "Hey, kids! Dessert!"

"That's Mom," I said with relief. "We better slide."

"I guess," Abe said reluctantly. "We'll be seeing you, Impossumble."

"Yeah, good night."

There was no answer. We both stood on tiptoe to peer at her hunched form on the branch above us. And then I heard it distinctly—a rusty little snore. "You bored her to sleep," I giggled. "What a conversationalist. You're never going to live it down!"

"Oh, shut up," Abe said.

75

9

The following week, Mom began shopping for our school clothes. The Philippines is a tropical country. Now we needed everything: hats, coats, boots, sweaters. We went to the mall and splurged.

The temperature was still in the nineties, and we ran the air-conditioning day and night. So it felt very strange to shop in stores crammed full of winter clothes. I tried on a turtleneck, with a woolly blue sweater on top, and a pleated plaid skirt. "A green coat for you, Rianne," Shannon said with authority. For someone so small she has very firm ideas about color.

When I shrugged the coat on I stared at my reflections in the three-way mirror. For years I had been wearing shorts and T-shirts and sandals in the tropics. Now a stranger looked at me from out of the glass. With her chubby, tanned knees covered and the baby fat sleeked down by the trendy sweater, she looked quite grown up. She might even need to wear a bra someday. Sometimes I think it's not natural, to grow and change. Life would be easier if you could get used to yourself before you alter. Even adults feel it—

76

they're always saying, "How you've grown! The last time I looked, you were just a baby!"

When we got home, loaded with shopping bags, Dad teased, "You better buy another lottery ticket, Rianne! I'll be a poor man before your mom is done!"

After dinner I hauled my stuff upstairs and sat down with a pair of nail scissors to cut off the tags and store labels. The socks and tights went into baskets in my closet, and the sweaters onto the shelf. I had just clipped off a price tag from a pair of pants when something soft and solid hit the window.

I started, and stared at the uncurtained glass, which had rattled a bit but showed no crack or mark. Something white was waving back and forth outside. Immediately all the ghost stories that Abe has ever told me rushed into my head. My heart began to jump up and down against my throat. The eerie shape suddenly jerked closer. I backed towards the door, ready to scream.

For a second the pale figure pressed against the glass. It was the Impossumble! The soft thumping sound came from her pink paws rapping on the window screen. The Impossumble had climbed to the very tip of a tall sapling in the backyard. When she swayed it close, she could just reach the window.

Hurriedly I slid the window up. The Impossumble fell against the screen again and clung there. "Let me in! My claws will give out!"

"Let me take down the other screen." I didn't dare try to wrench out the one the Impossumble held on to. Luckily the two windows in my room are side by

side, separated only by their frames. Kneeling on the desk, I opened the other window. The window screen popped out after I wrestled with it. I had to ruin my nail scissors to pry up the edge of the frame. The Impossumble kept up a running commentary of complaints, commands, and advice. But once the screen was down she swung over and dropped gratefully down into my room.

"It's so much easier to meet an animal acquaintance," she grumbled. "Everyone in the woods has a daily routine, a certain place at a certain time. But people! Turning night into day, rushing around in smelly metal machines—they brought a horrible yellow one into the forest the other day."

"I'm glad you came to visit me, Impossumble," I said, not entirely truthfully. If I want to hear whining and complaints I have a brother and a sister, after all!

I couldn't guess what the Impossumble wanted. She wouldn't go to all this trouble to visit me just for the pleasure of it. But I knew that asking questions would get me a cross comment. So I kept myself busy putting my new clothes away while the Impossumble morosely surveyed my room.

"Ugh, is this fake grass on the floor? Why is it the color of dying grass? You let that cat up here, I can smell it. Your bed is very high off the ground. What is this vine here? Oh, it's a wire! Something red is moving inside this box at the end of it. Is it a cage?"

I explained that it was a clock, the moving things inside being the red digital numbers. But I couldn't make the Impossumble understand what clocks measure. I had never thought before how abstract the

79

concept of time is. "I suppose animals never need to deal with things like that," I said. "Only things you can really touch, or taste, or smell matter."

"Or see or hear," the Impossumble agreed.

It occurred to me that one thing none of the talking-animal books ever went into was these basic questions. And here I was, talking to an opossum as well as Dr. Dolittle ever did. So the Impossumble would never help change the world. I could still find out, say, whether opossums believed in life after death, or how they thought the world began. Dad says that the yen to find out things for the mere sake of knowing them is what makes a reporter or a researcher. For the first time I understood what he meant. I didn't even want to write a paper or article about how opossums think. I just wanted to know.

In a fever of excitement I grabbed a pencil and a piece of paper. But just then the Impossumble decided to get down to business. "I have a reason for visiting you," she announced.

"You do? What is it?"

The Impossumble had climbed up onto my desk, and now sat up on her haunches. She wrinkled her pointed nose and sighed, as if words were an intolerable burden. "I kept thinking about what you said."

"What I said," I prompted, frantically casting my mind back.

"You know—about behaving nicely to other folks."

"Oh, that!"

"How I dislike dealing with people!" the Impossumble burst out irrelevantly. "These things are totally unimportant in the woods. If you meet another animal you either eat it or get eaten. Or you ignore each other. Life is so simple!"

I thought I spotted a mistake here. "What about those acquaintances with the regular habits?" I asked.

"I ignore them," she said. "But once you start talking with people, you have to learn their rules. I hate it." The Impossumble glared at me.

She seemed, even for the Impossumble, quite cross and upset. "You're an animal, you don't have to," I said soothingly.

"Oh, yes, I do," the Impossumble said bitterly. "You've been really nice to me. And I haven't been nice to you. I don't want to feel bad about it, but I do. It's all your fault."

All I could think of in my own defense was, "Well, I didn't mean to." After a pause I went on, "And I think you've been very nice to us. What about all those pieces of luck?"

"That's just it. You didn't think you were getting something for nothing, did you?" The Impossumble upended my can of pens and markers and began to examine each one without really looking at them. "An animal learns as a kit, or a pup, or whatever, that nothing is free. But I suppose people haven't advanced so far yet."

"Yes, we have," I said. "There's even a poster that says there's no such thing as a free lunch." A little chilly, worried feeling was creeping over me. "Are you saying those bits of luck were dangerous?"

"No—just unlucky." From the bottom of my pencil can the Impossumble fished out a piece of gray poster putty, encrusted with black pencil dust and eraser crumbs. She squeezed it experimentally between her pink, handlike paws. "Luck is like this thing, whatever it is. You can push it in on one side, and it squidges out on the other."

"Every action has an equal and opposite reaction," I remembered from science class.

"That's very well put," the Impossumble said. "Equal and opposite. That's right. When I gave you a bit of luck, I just borrowed it from someplace else in your life."

"You're trying to say we're going to have some *bad* luck. To balance our good." I was horrified. "Can't you *do* something about it?"

"I wish you would listen carefully to what I say," the Impossumble snapped. "Of course I could do something. But it would just make things worse in the end. Anything I did would just squidge your luck further out of shape. Sooner or later, you'd still have to pay."

"When will it be? What will happen?"

"How would I know?" The Impossumble climbed onto the window sill again, shaking her back legs fastidiously like a cat when it steps into a puddle. "You can open this window again. I just wanted to let you know—because you've been nice."

Stunned, I hauled the screenless window up. The Impossumble paused. "I'm, um, sorry about it. I should have told you right off."

I could see she wanted me to say something reassuring. "I'm sure it'll be okay," I lied.

The Impossumble's look was full of skepticism. "It's really not good for either of us to get friendly with each other," she said. "But—oh, well! I hope we can still be acquaintances."

"Sure," I said automatically. The Impossumble jumped like a squirrel out into the night. I heard a few rustling branches and cracking twigs, but nothing like what you might expect in the way of crashing weights and thumping bodies. I guess a small animal like an opossum can jump one full story without much trouble.

In books I've read about people wringing their hands. For the first time I felt like trying it. But I slammed the window down again instead, and hurried downstairs.

"You're just in time to help hand around dessert," Mom greeted me. "Poached peaches and ice cream."

I took a dish in each hand and carried them out into the living room. As I gave Dad a bowl he said, "Did I hear you open your window, Rianne? Be sure it's shut again, will you—we're running the A.C."

"Sure, Dad." Abe and Shannon were watching a miniseries on TV with total concentration. I went to put a bowl in Abe's hand and whispered, "Abe, can I tell you something?"

The rat didn't even look around! He just said, "Move along, squirt. I'm busy."

I went back to the kitchen, seething, and carried in two more dishes of ice cream. Mom brought in her own. I gave one to Shannon, who didn't look up, either. Then I sat on the sofa and waited for a commercial. For some reason it took ages. I ate some ice cream and peaches, but hardly tasted it as it went down.

Finally, a trio of ladies in spangled tights and top hats came on, singing about Dodge dealerships. I leaned forward and nudged Abe again. "Let's see if there's another peach."

"Good idea."

I knew there was one more peach, because Mom always prepares fruit in half dozens. I ran into the kitchen ahead of Abe and grabbed the pot, where the last peach was cooling in its poaching syrup. I held the lid on with my other hand and turned to face my brother. "Listen to me for a second, Abe."

"Hey, Ree! Be fair, and split it!"

I wanted to hit him, but didn't dare let go of either pot or lid. "Abe! *Listen* to me!"

"What?" he said impatiently.

"I talked to the Impossumble just now."

"So she stays awake for you, huh?" Abe took the vanilla ice cream out of the freezer and began to scoop it. "How are we going to strike it rich next?"

"We're not! Abe, that luck wasn't free. We have to pay for it!"

"We do? How?"

"With some compensating bad fortune."

Abe flopped the ice cream carton shut. "It doesn't sound very likely on the face of it, Ree. Are you sure the Impossumble knows what she's talking about? She's only an animal."

"Abe, how can you say that? She must know what she's dealing with. When she helped you meet Amber Doherty she wasn't only an animal!"

That was a big tactical mistake. At the sound of Amber's name Abe's face became like wood. Without another word he grabbed his dish and hustled back into the living room. He didn't even wait to wrestle the peach from me. So I ate it, and some more ice cream, too. I sat at the kitchen table and tried to convince myself that nothing would happen, that everything would be okay. What could Abe have done about it? If the Impossumble was right, there was nothing anyone could do.

What I really wanted was intelligent sympathy and understanding. I had to make do with Shannon. After the miniseries had reeled its way to a cliff-hanger, I marched into Shannon's room.

Mom's new regime extended to our rooms. Everyone had to make their beds and dust. If you didn't do it, it wouldn't get done. Mom would vacuum your floor every Wednesday if you picked it up beforehand. Clean sheets would appear in your room but you had to put them onto the bed.

To Shannon this meant she didn't have to do anything at all. As I picked my way into her room, the dust bunnies skittered over the paint samples and felt-tip pens on the floor. Every inch of her desk, nightstand, and windowsill was cluttered with junk—pinecones she meant to glue together into wreaths, half-empty glasses, little blocks of wood that were someday going to have windows and doors marked on, crumpled tissues stained with paint. A limp spider plant cutting drooped in a dry jar on the sill. As I passed, I transferred it into a mug that held half an inch of watery iced tea. To a parched plant I should think tea tastes good.

Shannon sat in her pajamas on the gritty, gray

sheets of her bed, reading an Archie comic. Without looking up she said, "Leave my plant alone, Ree."

I perched gingerly on the edge of the bed, and half a vanilla wafer fell to the rug. "Yick! How can you sleep in this? The crumbs are ground in!"

"I might want to eat it later," Shannon said, as if that kind of forethought was the most natural thing in the world.

I shuddered. About some things Shannon has no nerves whatever. To other things, though, she's very sensitive indeed. By the time I finished repeating my talk with the Impossumble to her, she had dropped the comic book. "Oh, my God, Rianne!" she whimpered when I was done. "This is awful, something dreadful's going to happen!"

"I don't see any way out of it," I agreed unhappily.

Tears gathered under Shannon's long, brown eyelashes. Her little pixie face looked like one of those stupid paintings of big-eyed kids you see in tacky restaurants. "Could it—could it be even worse than when the car crashed?"

I was suddenly appalled by my own stupidity. Now Shannon would never be able to fall asleep. She would lie awake all night thinking of more and more disastrous things that might happen. Worse, she might creep to my room to wake me and tell me about them. But in all honesty I had to answer, "I don't know, Shannon."

"I wish we'd never rescued that opossum!" she cried. Then she threw herself onto the pillow and burst into tears.

"Maybe it won't be that terrible," I tried to comfort her.

But she dragged the covers over her head. From beneath came her muffled howl, "Go away, Rianne! Everything's horrible! I wish we'd stayed in the Philippines!" So I gave up and tiptoed out. I nearly broke my ankle stepping on an empty soda can.

ᕫ10ᕫ

The rest of that week was terrible. Shannon didn't sleep a wink and as a result had purple rings under her eyes the next morning. I hadn't slept well, either, though my sister hadn't actually woken me. So we were both visibly out of sorts at breakfast. Mom became alarmed and felt our foreheads. "I can't feel any fever," she worried. "Abe, run up and get the thermometer from the cabinet upstairs, will you?"

"There's nothing wrong with me, Mom," I protested, jerking my head away from her cool hand.

"What about you, baby? Do you hurt anywhere?"

Mom rubbed the back of Shannon's neck gently. I gave my sister a sharp glance, worried that she would blurt out everything. But all Shannon did was shut her eyes. "My head hurts a little," she said.

Abe came clattering back downstairs with the thermometer. Naturally our temperatures were normal. Mom took our immunization records from Dad's desk drawer. These are yellow booklets which the doctor stamps or writes in after he inoculates you. To live in the Philippines we had to have shots for about a hundred diseases, because it's a tropical country.

When I look through my booklet I'm always impressed with my own bravery. How very many diseases there are, and I've been stuck for every one!

But Shannon's mind works differently. Now, as she flipped through her booklet, she imagined herself getting yellow fever, or typhus, or cholera. Her face got paler and more pinched every second.

And Mom found an even more nerve-racking warning in the fine print on the back. After urging the patient to keep his booklet with his passport, it went on to warn that some foreign diseases take a long time to surface. If you got sick after coming back from certain places—the countries were listed, and seemed to run from Afghanistan to Zimbabwe—you should consider consulting a specialist.

"I don't feel good," Shannon whimpered.

Mom felt her forehead again. "It won't do you any harm to spend a quiet day," she said. "Do you feel like going back to bed? I'll tuck you in. And I'll make you some chicken soup."

When Mom saw Shannon's room, she sent Abe and me to the store on our bikes to buy some chicken backs for soup while she picked up some of the mess. Mom would never give in like that to Abe or me. Just because she's the youngest, Shannon gets away with murder. It was another grilling hot day, and as we labored up the hill to the shopping center Abe said, "You and your big mouth. Maybe the runt will actually make herself ill, and that'll be our bad luck!"

"Oh, I hope not! And you were the one who told me not to be so secretive—I'm not going to listen to you anymore."

And of course, after a little nap, Shannon felt fine. All her fuss served no purpose, unless you count irritating the family and making Abe and me nervous.

For several days we wandered around the house like lost souls, waiting for disaster to strike. It's funny how much heavier an impending *bad* event feels. When we were hanging around waiting for a bit of good luck we looked forward to a surprise, something light and brightly colored that would suddenly pop like a piñata and sprinkle us with goodies. Now it was as if a large metal weight hovered invisibly somewhere just overhead. It got so on our nerves, Abe and I even discussed making a clean breast of the whole business to Mom and Dad. But, as Abe pointed out, nothing had happened yet. So we decided to let it slide for a while.

And, like before, we got used to it. I gave up worrying about it by the weekend, not because I had figured out a way to avert trouble, but simply from boredom. Other things happened.

Some fall seed-and-bulb catalogs came in the mail. Shannon and I helped Dad plan a very ambitious spring garden. When we lived in Manila, the gardener took care of everything. Now, in an ecstasy of suburban enthusiasm, Dad bought some grass food and a spreader. He and Abe spent all one afternoon fertilizing and seeding the grass, and then sprinkling it.

There was a movie at the church Friday night for young people, and with Shannon egging me on I tagged along with Abe. Mom drove us both there, so he couldn't think of a good excuse to get out of it. Of course, he wouldn't sit with me, and all the kids there were high schoolers, a lot older than me. But I actually met Amber Doherty! Rev. Watterton's wife introduced us. But then Abe swooped down and zoomed off with her. In the car on the way home I remembered Mom's request, and was very restrained. I asked Abe only one casual question, about where Amber lived. The way he glared at me, you would have thought I wanted to know if she murdered people with a machine gun in her spare time.

On Saturday afternoon Jane got into a horrific fight with a black cat from down the street. They yelled cat cuss words at each other, and rolled back and forth on the sidewalk clawing tufts of fur out of each other. Abe argued that Jane should learn to defend the homestead, while Shannon worried that both animals would kill each other. Mom was on Shannon's side, saying, "We don't want Jane to get wounded and have to go to the vet."

Abe said, "Yeah, but how can anybody stop it?" The cats had paused briefly, chest to chest and eye to eye, to exchange growls and rude comments. Then they started in again. The fight looked just like the ones in cartoons, with the combatants rolling over and over in a blurred mass. The tufts of black fur and orange-and-white fur literally flew, drifting around the driveway like snow.

"Turn on the hose," Mom commanded. At the first spatter of water the fight broke up. With a flurry of claws, Jane scurried up a tree. Her opponent took to his heels. We let Jane calm down for a few hours, and then coaxed her down with the help of a sardine. Both Shannon and I looked her over, stroking her fur and feeling her paws. But we couldn't find any wounds from the fight. "It was all bark and no bite," Shannon said, disappointed. "Except for the tufts of fur." She had hoped to practice being a vet by binding up Jane's injuries.

The weather had been very hot and muggy. There was a pattern to it, several humid scorchers and then, just when no one could stand it anymore, a violent thunderstorm in the late afternoon or evening. Late Sunday the black clouds began to pile up in the sky. The hot air was still and tense, like a patient in a dentist's chair. Finally a few big raindrops began to fall, and a sudden wind tossed the treetops. A tremendous crack of thunder, and the rain began to cascade down.

Safe in our air-conditioned comfort, we hardly noticed the storm at first. Mom was trying out a new recipe for beef. Abe had a tennis tournament on TV. Jane slept on his lap. Shannon was reading *Misty of Chincoteague,* and I was helping Dad to clean a gun.

Or I was trying to, anyway, because he doesn't often let me handle a gun or its ammunition. But after he took it apart, I helped him oil the bits and rub them with a greasy cloth. When the only guns you touch are toy ones, you kind of expect a real gun to be fairly light. It always surprises me how heavy a real gun is in your hand. I'm the only one who's inherited any interest in Dad's work. I can tell he has mixed feelings about that, too. But today he didn't bother repeating that police work is ninety-five percent boredom and five percent pure terror. Instead he showed me how to disassemble a revolver. Even our hands are alike, square and stubby fingered, and pretty soon we had black oil all over them.

Then all of a sudden the lights went out. Abe yelped in agony as the TV picture dwindled away into a blue pinpoint of light. Mom said, "Oh dear, and I haven't put the carrots in yet." In the sudden quiet we could hear the howling wind and the rain lashing on the roof.

More quickly than I thought possible Dad fitted the revolver together again. "As soon as I clean this up I'll set up some candles," he promised Mom.

I watched his hands dart around without a single wasted motion, quickly and neatly fitting together the deadly little gun. "When I join the Marine Corps, will they teach me to be that quick?" I asked.

I had only decided to become a marine last night, but Dad didn't sound surprised. "Sure," he said. "But it'll be a few years yet before the marines can recruit you. In the meantime, hands off!" I nodded obediently. Dad's always emphasized that firearms are a dangerous tool, not for ignorant or irresponsible people to play with.

"There's no air-conditioning now, so let's open some windows," Mom said. Abe slid open the door onto the deck, and a cool breeze whispered in. It smelled of rain and green leaves.

The thunder muttered sullenly in the distance. And then, very clearly, we all heard a slow tearing sound, like a hundred pencils being broken. There was a tremendous crash that made the entire house shake. The sliding glass door in front of me cracked diagonally as I watched, and Mom's cookbooks slid off their shelf to the floor.

Mom hugged a clean copper saucepan, her mouth open. Jane hissed and darted under the sofa. We kids wasted time and energy running around and yelling, "Oh, what is it?" or "Is it a nuclear war, Mom?" or "Something's attacking us!"

But Dad is trained for crisis situations. In the blink of an eye he was running like a jackrabbit for the stairs. We surged after him, chattering like idiots, but Mom cut us off and made us go back. "Abe, find the flashlights. Rianne, wipe that oil off your hands, this minute. Shannon, keep back."

"It's nothing much, Irene," Dad called from upstairs. "Annoying, but not too dangerous. There's a tree fallen into our bedroom."

"A tree!" Now we did race up the stairs. Abe had found the two flashlights we keep in the garage. Dad took charge of the big, powerful red one, and let us kids fight over the plastic penlight. There was a huge, jagged hole in the roof, in the corner of the big bedroom. Half the room was open to the sky. A big broken tree limb poked right through it to scrape the floor. There were wet brown leaves everywhere. The rain poured in like a flood, soaking the green carpet and driving in onto the bed. Dad grabbed the mattress, covers and all, and dragged it clear.

"We can get the box spring," Abe volunteered.

"No, I don't want you kids going near that hole," Dad said. "Here, you take this and drag it into Rianne's room."

Abe and I did. Shannon carried the pillows. The blankets and sheets were wet, and we pulled them off, but the mattress underneath was dry. By that time

Dad had moved the box spring into the hall. We put that in Abe's room.

"What about the clothes? And the books?" Mom asked. The closet, which was built across the end of the room, was smashed open. Dad's end, with the gun cabinet, was okay, but all Mom's clothes were under the hole, getting wet.

"We're going to have to let that ride, Irene," Dad said. "I can't open what's left of the closet door—the tree's jammed it down too hard. But the books we can save." He took them out of the shattered bookcase. We carried them downstairs into the dining room and laid them out to dry.

Mom brought up a stepladder and a big roll of plastic trash bags. She and Dad tried to cover the hole from the rain, by thumbtacking garbage bags around the tree and over the hole. But it was impossible, the way the wind blew and the tree leaned into the hole. Of course, not only was it raining cats and dogs all this time, but there was no light. Abe and I took turns holding the flashlights for them until Dad said, "This is hopeless. Let's set out buckets and pans on the floor to catch the water."

Mom spread the garbage bags over the squishy-wet carpet, a more disgusting green than ever now that it was soaked. We carried up every container in the house—trash cans, buckets, jars, trays, flowerpot saucers, everything. We laid them rim to rim under the hole, and balanced open umbrellas over the areas we couldn't cover.

"There's a big wet stain spreading over the ceiling downstairs," Dad warned. "Fix it up as best you can, and then let's keep out of here. The floor may be weakened."

We were all soaking wet. Mom made us change. "What about you and Dad?" Shannon demanded.

"We have underwear and socks," Mom said soothingly. "I can run our clothes through the dryer when the electricity comes back." Meanwhile, she borrowed my bathrobe, and Dad wore Abe's.

The rain slashed down like a monsoon, casting its gloomy spell over what remained of the day. There was nothing for dinner, because the stove had no electricity to finish cooking the beef. The sky grew too dark for anyone to read, and all we had to watch was the big, dark water stain spreading over the dining room ceiling. Dad phoned his favorite pizza carryout, and learned that their electric ovens were out, too. Mom got out the Yellow Pages and found a Chinese restaurant that did deliveries in Reston. "Good," said Dad solemnly. "I don't fancy going out into this rain in nothing but Abe's bathrobe." We all had to laugh at that. Abe is as tall as Dad but maybe about one-fifth as wide. His bathrobe had to sort of stretch around Dad's middle, and there was a wide uncovered stripe down Dad's front.

The flashlight batteries were getting weak, so I brought out the company candlesticks. They were beautiful, silverplated all up their three tall branches. Mom found the candles she used to use at embassy dinners. The yellow light they cast was much less bright than electric lamps. The candle flames moved a little in the draft, and made funny shadows crawl in the corners of the room. The kitchen no longer looked like our kitchen.

Everyone felt better when the food came. Mom had ordered shrimp lo mein, our favorite, plus a lot of spicy dishes for herself and Dad. "Tomorrow," Dad said, "we'll call the landlady. She'll get the tree down, and the roof fixed."

"Can everything be put back okay?" Shannon wanted to know. "How long will it take? Can we repaint the bedroom blue?"

"I don't see why not," Mom said. "They'll certainly have to repaint it."

"Oh, goody! I'll choose a color for you!"

"That's not all they'll have to repaint," Dad said, glancing up at the ceiling. "After dinner's cleared away I think we should move this table. The water may drip through."

While Shannon and I rinsed off the dishes in cold water, to save what hot water there was for baths, Abe and Dad moved all the dining room furniture into the living room. What with the table and the six chairs there was hardly room to turn around there. The house felt all rumpled and uncomfortable, like a gym sock scrunched down around the heel of your tennis shoe. "I think we might as well all go to bed," Dad said.

It was sort of an adventure, brushing our teeth and getting ready for bed by candlelight, but only Shannon really enjoyed it. As we carried our candles around Mom followed us. "Don't put them near any curtains," she warned. "Don't hold papers or books near the flame."

"I don't know how they managed in George Washington's time," Abe grumbled.

97

"And don't knock the candles over."

"Why not?" I said. "They would just go out."

"It would be very easy to start a fire that way," Mom pointed out.

"Oh!" And all of a sudden I found myself balancing my candle in its saucer very carefully indeed. Our run of bad luck surely wasn't over yet.

❧ 11 ❧

In one sense, the tree was well timed. It fell in mid-August. If school were in session, and if Mom had begun her graduate courses, life would have been completely impossible. As it was, we all had to work like beavers. No one complained anymore of there not being anything to do!

The insurance man came. A tree man came, but couldn't cut the tree down right away because his crew was in Leesburg on another job. The landlady came, bringing a roof man who couldn't start patching the roof until the tree man took away the tree. A woman came from the power company to be sure no electric cables were involved in the accident. In the daylight, the dining-room ceiling looked awful, sagging like rotten cloth around the ugly fake-colonial chandelier. A man who did drywall came to give an estimate on fixing it.

And Mrs. Hernandez came over. Mom and I sat on the deck with her while she apologized over and over again for the bad manners of her daughter's tree. "Time and again I've reminded Joseph to have it taken down," she said. "That tree! It's been haunting my nightmares ever since the gypsy moths killed it two years ago! I always thought it would fall on us, the way it leaned."

"It was just bad luck that the wind pushed it our way," Mom said.

Shannon and I looked at each other but didn't say anything for a moment. Then I whispered to her, "You know, there's one good thing about this. We can be sure that Bobby Canfield will get a fair shake, too."

"That's right!" Shannon brightened up visibly. Bobby Canfield represented the piece of this whole Impossumble summer that bothered her the most. "Maybe he'll win the Reader's Digest Sweep."

"Or be nominated to the Supreme Court when he's fifty," I said. "Or win a Nobel Prize for physics."

"Or get a date with Brooke Shields."

"He must be only a little kid," I protested, laughing. "Brooke Shields is too old for him."

From the open windows above came the roar of the wet-vacuum. Dad had gone out and rented it first thing in the morning. Then he had had to go to work. So Abe had been given the job of vacuuming up the water from the carpet.

"And now your roof is broken," Mrs. Hernandez mourned. "I'm so sorry!"

"Is the rest of your family due back soon?" Mom asked politely.

"Before school starts they'll be back. And I'll send Louise right over, dear. She's just Rianne's age. The darling twins are a little younger than your youngest," Mrs. Hernandez added. "But perhaps Shannon wouldn't play with little boys much, anyway." Shannon made a face, but she wasn't in Mrs. Hernandez's line of vision, so it was okay.

In the afternoon, the tree man came back with a truckload of ropes, ladders, and assistants. It was very interesting to watch them carve up the tree with chain saws, and drag the chunks clear with thick ropes. Before they began I couldn't imagine how the tree could be cut up without crashing down, maybe onto the deck. But the workmen made it look easy. "You got some nice dry firewood here, ma'am," one workman said to Mom.

"Do you need firewood?" Mom phoned to ask Mrs. Hernandez. "It's your tree, after all."

"Dear, I think you should keep any usable wood," Mrs. Hernandez said. "It's the least I can give you." So Mom had them cut the wood up, and we stacked the logs in the backyard.

By that time it was too late to begin fixing the roof. Mom and Abe tacked plastic over the hole to keep out leaves and squirrels. After being wet-vacked all day the carpet was nearly dry. You could feel the wetness deep down in the pile if you walked on it barefoot, but at least every step didn't squish. With all the leaves and twigs cleaned up, we could almost pretend the room was normal again. So we moved the bed back in, and made it.

Now that the tree was gone, the closet could be opened. Mom took all the wet clothes off the hangers and sorted them into dryer loads. We lined up the shoes on the deck so the sunshine could dry them and kill any mildew. "Thank goodness I have a sensible wardrobe," Mom said. "Hardly anything is really ruined."

It took days to get the house back together, what with replacing the dining-room ceiling and reroofing the bedroom. We would have been more involved in the work, especially Shannon, except for what happened next. On Wednesday morning after the big storm the phone rang and I answered it. It was Abe.

"Hi, I thought you were playing in that tennis tournament," I said. Tennis players in this area are ranked—everyone knows who's best, who's second best, and so on. Since Abe just moved here he didn't have a ranking yet. But he had already won two matches, so he'd have one next year.

"Put Mom on," he said.

I had never heard Abe use that sort of tone before—weak but rigid. "What's up?" I asked, a little scared.

"I'm calling from the hospital," he said. "I think I've broken my ankle."

"Abe! No! How did you do it?"

"I just stepped off a curb," he said impatiently. "Now put Mom on, will you? They can't fix it unless she gives consent."

Quickly I called Mom. When she hung up she looked a little dazed, and leaned her forehead on the wall next to the phone. "Let me come with you to the hospital, Mom!" I begged.

"No, Rianne." She straightened up. "I'd rather you stay here, and let in the drywall man. He's coming before lunch, and I doubt they'll be done with Abe by then."

"Then take Shannon with you," I pleaded, and

Mom was so preoccupied she agreed. I galloped up the stairs and burst into Shannon's room.

"I think yellow is the best for the master bedroom after all," Shannon announced. "How do you like this one—Lemon Haze?" She waved a paint chip.

"Never mind that," I said. "Abe's at the hospital with a bum ankle, and Mom's driving over now. You're going with her."

"Oh, poor Abie! But why do I have to go?"

I shoved my face close to hers. "Because of that Impossumble," I almost hissed at her. "That bad luck isn't over yet by a long shot, I'm sure of it. Mom's worried and distracted enough. *You* keep an eye on how fast she's driving, and on the traffic. Remember that auto accident!"

Shannon gulped and nodded, pale as oatmeal. She put on her sneakers and silently followed Mom out to the car. Alone in the house, I couldn't sit still. I paced round and round, upstairs and down, thinking.

As Abe had said, we got a boost of wealth, health, and happiness from the Impossumble. It seemed that our compensating downturns were running the same way. Mom and Dad hadn't discussed it with us, but I knew that this tree episode had been expensive. The landlady's and our renters' insurance didn't cover everything. And Abe's physical well-being had sure taken a shellacking today. When I thought about how our happiness might be in danger, I could have screamed. I had to argue myself out of the idea of going down the hill and asking the Impossumble to give things another tweak again. I knew that would just cause more trouble in the end.

The drywall man came and began work. Repairing the dining-room ceiling had halted for a long time at the most revolting stage, with the ruined drywall all cut away. A huge heap of torn wet hunks had already been hauled away, but there were still plenty more. In the gaping hole you could see bare rafters and the underside of the master-bedroom floor. The hole had to stay open for a week to let the underside dry out some. "You got another box for these bits?" the workman asked.

"Sure," I went down to the basement and brought up a big one. The sight of all those boxes neatly stacked up inspired me. Instead of wasting time worrying, I decided to act the way you're supposed to in the U.S., and Do It Myself.

I opened a can of soup for lunch. Then I thought about fixing dinner. There were some pieces of lamb marinating in a bowl of wine in the fridge, but I didn't want to mess with any of Mom's creations. I found some green beans to wash and cut up. And I took a package of chicken legs from the freezer. Dad could always broil those on the grill. There were potatoes, so I peeled them all and made a big potato salad. And I tried very hard all the time not to listen for the car coming back.

At last, when the afternoon was practically over, I heard the car back down the driveway into the garage. I dropped the paring knife into the sink and hurried out. Mom looked exhausted, and Shannon chattered like a monkey. With her, that means she's nervous and upset. "Boy, Rianne, you should have seen that hospital!" she exclaimed. "I don't know why there were so many emergencies today. There was even a boy with a tick, can you believe it? It was stuck onto his head, and his mom couldn't get it off."

Very carefully Abe manipulated his foot out. It was all wrapped up in beige and white bandages at the end of his long bony shin, like something in a war movie. Mom helped him balance on his good leg, and Shannon took some crutches out of the back. Abe hobbled shakily through into the kitchen. "Oh, Abe!" I said. "Does it hurt much?"

"Oh no, not at all!" he snarled.

"But it's not broken, Ree, isn't that lucky?" Shannon gabbled. "It's just a very bad sprain. They put a brace on it, and a lot of elastic bandages, but it's not a real plaster cast."

"I began dinner," I told Mom.

"Oh, Rianne, thank you, what a relief." Mom set her purse down on the kitchen table and sat down. "May I never go through an afternoon like this again!" She took off her glasses and rubbed her eyes.

From the most comfortable armchair in the living room Abe called, "I want a drink."

"Try saying please, Mr. Invalid," I said, when I brought him a soda.

The ankle hurt a lot, of course, and for such an active guy it was hard for Abe to have to sit still. But even taking all these things into consideration, Abe was a terrible patient. He grumped about being too hot or too cold. He always needed things that were upstairs when he was down, or downstairs after he hobbled up. His blanket weighed too heavily on his foot when he went to bed, so Mom had to search out

105

the thinnest one in the house and remake his bed. He hated all the books in the house, but couldn't think of anything he might like me to bring him from the library. And if he watched TV, someone had to always be hopping up to change the channel for him. Shannon begged Dad to buy a TV with remote control, but he said it was too expensive for such a short-term illness. "Abe only has to wear the brace for three weeks," Dad pointed out.

I guess worst of all, from Abe's point of view—even worse than not being able to play tennis—was that he couldn't hang around with Amber. The doctors told him to keep off his leg as much as possible for a few weeks. He couldn't even go to church on Sunday, never mind the midweek youth group.

Instead, he had to phone her. That had its problems, too, since there are two phones in the house—one in the kitchen and one in the big bedroom. Abe would go into the bedroom and shut the door to phone. Then he would interrupt himself at least twice every time, to yell down the stairs, "Is anyone on the extension?"

And everyone downstairs would chorus, "No!" So he'd be reassured—for a little while!

Mom kept an eye on us when Abe did this, but actually Shannon and I were very good. When Amber came by to visit Abe, we couldn't help feeling it was the reward of keeping our bratty inclinations under firm restraint. The moment I answered the door I felt insane giggles rising up in my chest. There was no reason at all for it, because all Amber said was, "Hi! Is Abe home? I brought him some cupcakes."

106

"He's in the living room," I said in a muffled voice, and pointed out the way. Shannon was in the kitchen, and we stayed there giggling and whispering idiotic comments to each other. After she left, Abe hobbled in and yelled, "Being the oldest in this family is like confinement in a loony bin!"

Amazingly, poor Amber wasn't grossed out by her first visit. She came again with a few friends the next week. With other teenagers there, we younger ones felt more serious. We brought out Trivial Pursuit, and it was lots more fun with so many players.

⁓12⁓

The next day was a Friday. Dad had to work late. Mom took the opportunity to make lamb curry, which Dad doesn't enjoy. Scrumptious Indian smells were filling the whole house when I turned on the TV. Abe usually hogs it, but this afternnon he had dragged himself out onto the deck to read the latest issue of *Sports Illustrated*. Our TV is so old, the sound comes on long before the picture.

"—tense situation. The authorities have cordoned off 23rd Street, and as you can see, State Department employees are being evacuated from the building. I have here Mrs. Cecilia Fort, who works in the Passport Division—"

"Mom!" I called. "Something's going on at Daddy's office!"

With agonizing slowness the picture took shape on the screen. A blow-dried reporter was interviewing a fluttery old filing clerk. Mom came in, a knife in one hand and *Chanson de Roland* in the other. "What is it?" she asked absently. "A bomb threat?"

Then we both stared at the TV, transfixed. It showed a fairly long shot of the State Department's entrance.

There's a sort of marquee to keep the rain off while diplomats hail their taxis, and several massive concrete benches and planters to keep suicide bombers from driving up. And there was Dad! His big, square body was perfectly visible just inside the thick glass entrance doors. I even recognized the expression on his face— mulish and stubborn but thinking very hard, the sort of look he had when the lawn spreader jammed and he had to unjam it. Just visible a ways behind him was a man with a ski mask over his head. He was pointing a long gun at Dad's back.

I know I screamed, because Abe and Shannon came hurrying into the room. Mom put the paring knife carefully on top of the TV and turned the sound way up. "—sent a hostage out to present a list of de-

mands," the reporter blared. As we watched, Dad slowly turned and walked back into the building. The police outside couldn't shoot at the gunman for fear of hitting Dad.

Shannon began to sob. "What will happen to Daddy?"

"Abe, I want you to sit and watch the TV very carefully," Mom said in a quiet voice. "Rianne, go into the dining room and turn on the radio. Find the all-news station. I'm going to make some phone calls."

"There won't be anyone at the office, Mom," I said, gulping down my tears. "They're evacuating the building."

"There'll be somebody, somewhere." She rummaged around in the desk for the phone book.

As I passed the kitchen door the phone rang. Automatically I answered it. "Buechner residence."

"Hi, I'm Daniel Oberhauser with Channel Eight news. Are you Mrs. Irene Buechner?"

"No." I handed the phone to Mom.

She frowned for a moment and then said, "I have nothing to say. You must excuse me, I need this line." And she hung up. Immediately the phone rang again. This time she didn't even bother to talk to whoever it was. She just clicked the receiver for a second, to clear the line. Then quickly she picked it up and dialed out.

I found the all-news station on the radio. They were making a traffic report and cracking jokes. I was congratulating myself on being very brave and competent, when the tears rolled down my cheeks. If we lost Daddy, nothing could ever make up for it. I realized now how Bobby Canfield must have felt. Some losses are irreparable.

That evening seemed endless, like the weird dreams you get when you have a high fever. We forgot all about eating. As I passed the stove, I caught the smell of something beginning to burn, and turned the heat off. Mom made call after call, patient and frozen as a statue. Whenever she set the phone down, it would ring under her hand. She wouldn't speak to any callers. "What help would it be?" she said in a moment between calls. "It's lucky we live so far out in the suburbs. Otherwise we'd have reporters knocking at the door."

From TV and radio, and from the police or whoever Mom got hold of by phone, we learned that the trouble had started this afternoon. Some men had come into the State Department with a suitcase. When the security guard wanted to inspect it, they brought guns out of their pockets and shot him. The suitcase had a bomb in it, or so they said. As one of the security chiefs Dad organized the evacuation of the building. I knew without anyone saying it that Dad had let himself be taken hostage instead of someone else. With his training Dad would feel he had a better chance of surviving than some inexperienced bureaucrat or secretary. I just hoped his self-confidence was justified.

"But what's it all in aid of?" Abe burst out. The list of demands hadn't been very revealing, mostly requests for cigarettes and whatnot.

"What difference does it make?" Shannon had wept until her face looked like a pizza, all puffy and red.

"They're all lunatics. Remember that mental patient who broke the windshield of the German ambassador's car in Manila?"

"Maybe they want a political prisoner released," I said. "That's what terrorists in the Middle East always ask for. If we give them what they want—"

"The government never does," Abe said crushingly. "They've been burned too often on that one." And I knew it was true.

The doorbell rang. As I went to answer it Mom called, "Put up the chain first, Ree." I steeled myself to slam the door on some TV camera. I wanted to say something really vicious, maybe mentioning vultures, but the right comment wouldn't gel in my mind. Fastening the chain, I cracked the door open.

"Hello, Rianne—we thought you all might need some support." It was Amber Doherty. Stupefied, I undid the chain and let her in. On her heels came a short, chunky woman who cradled carefully in her arms a big flat pan covered with foil. "This is my mother," Amber said, and I mumbled something.

"You poor thing," Mrs. Doherty said briskly. "We saw it all on TV, and I realized you must be too frazzled to cook." And she marched on into the kitchen, where I heard her introducing herself to Mom.

"We brought lasagna," Amber said.

In no time Mrs. Doherty had the table set and the lasagna in the oven. "Amber will watch the TV while you eat," she told Abe. "And I'll sit here on hold on the telephone for you, Irene."

"I don't know how to thank you, Enid," Mom said faintly.

"In a crisis we all have to pull together," Mrs. Doherty said. "Oh, and before you sit down, Amber, run out and get the portable TV from the car. I brought ours," she added to Mom, "in case you wanted to watch two channels at once."

"That's a good idea," Abe said, a little awed.

"And this is wonderful lasagna," Shannon said, chewing.

It was. None of us had realized we were hungry, but after all, it was past ten o'clock. As the lasagna disappeared, I began to feel better, not optimistic, exactly, but fortified for events to come. It's amazing what a good meal can do.

After we ate, Amber helped me clear the dishes and wipe the table. She was so nice, I felt sorry I'd been so mean to Abe. Then Mom said, "I think it's time for you younger ones to go to bed. It's very late."

"But what if something happens?" Shannon cried.

"There's nothing you can do," Mom said firmly. "And you need your rest."

"I don't, Mom, not as much as Shannon," I begged. "Let me stay up, please? Just a little while longer?"

Mom looked more harassed than ever, and I almost took it back. But then, unexpectedly, Abe said. "Let her hang around a bit, Mom, please?"

I was amazed. Abe's the one who always complains that we younger kids are spoiled rotten. To hear him tell it, Mom and Dad acted like marine drill sergeants when he was a baby, and have become soft from old age. But I guess they are a little more lenient with us. Mom sighed and said, "All right, for just a few minutes. I'll come up with you, pumpkin, and tuck you in."

Amber wiped the kitchen counters and Mrs. Doherty set up the second TV in the dining room. Abe jerked his head at me and said, "C'mon, Ree." I followed him as he hobbled into the living room and collapsed into his chair. Our TV was still turned high, and two sitcom characters were loudly swapping wisecracks. I had to sit on the footstool and lean close to hear Abe speak. "Someone has to get hold of that Impossumble," he said softly.

"You know that won't do any good."

"I've been thinking about it," Abe said. "The luck the Impossumble talks about must be like a bank account. You know—money goes in and gets drawn out. The Impossumble is like one of those automatic money machines. She can let you get a lot of money out without going through the tellers."

"I get it," I said. "And if you draw too much money out, you have to get more before you can buy something else."

"That's right." Abe frowned at the television, which showed a bunch of people dancing on a beach and drinking diet 7-Up. "The Impossumble doesn't *create* luck. All we've done this summer is *borrow* luck, from the future. Like the way a credit card lets you borrow money to pay back later."

"And now it's time to pay it back." All of a sudden the whole horrible situation rushed in on me again, and I almost sobbed. "Oh, Abe! Suppose Dad gets shot or something?"

"Don't you see?" Abe set his chin, which gave him a look of Dad for a moment. "All this other stuff"— he gestured at his ankle—"we can live with. The roof

114

can be fixed. Mom can buy more clothes. My leg will get better. But if Dad dies . . ." He gulped, and dragged the back of his hand across his eyes. "We can't fix that. Ever. It would be a four-star calamity. You see what I'm saying? To pay back the debt bit by bit is okay. But this is too big a lump to pay all at once."

I thought hard. "What do people do if they can't pay their MasterCards? File for bankruptcy? Can we do that when we've borrowed luck?"

"Forget the MasterCard," Abe said. "What we have to do, what *you* have to do, is find that Impossumble. Tell her, well, that—"

"That we'll do anything to save Daddy's life," I finished for him. "But Abe, isn't that like, well, borrowing more money to pay your credit card off?"

"Of course it is," Abe snarled. "But as long as it's something we can survive, let her hit on as many unimportant things as she wants!"

It was the first time Abe had ever implied that tennis was of secondary importance, and I was really touched. Before I could say so, though, Mom came in. "Your turn now, Rianne," she said in a no-non-sense voice.

"Goodnight, Mom." I haven't done it in a while, but now I hugged her hard.

She stroked my hair. "Try to sleep, darling. Tomorrow will be here soon enough." I didn't think I could close my eyes, but I fell asleep the minute I hit the pillow.

13

The next morning I woke instantly, without any of the usual yawning and mumbling and slowly getting up to speed. I pulled on some clothes and hurried downstairs. It was very early. Mrs. Doherty sat dozing by the phone. Amber was gone. The TV was still on, showing cartoons, but very softly. Mom lay sleeping on the sofa, covered by the knitted afghan. I unlocked the front door and ran up the driveway for the newspaper. The asphalt felt rough and cool under my feet; the heat wave was over and rain hung in the air.

The newspaper was rolled up inside the box beneath the mailbox. It uncurled in my hands, revealing a bold black headline, "Liberation Group Seizes State Department." My stomach clenched into a hard lump of ice in my middle as I read it. Somehow, it's so much more serious when you see it in print.

A white paneled van that I had never seen before was parked across the street. A tall man got out and came over towards me. "Are you one of the Buechner children?" he asked. He said the name wrong, too.

I glared at him. "Who are you?"

"I'm a reporter with the American News Service," he began, smiling reassuringly. "If you're one of Donald Buechner's kids, I'd like to—"

"No, I'm not," I interrupted him. It was a real relief to get mad, to wash the cold, scary lump inside me away with a rush of words. "My name is Nancy. I'm an exchange student from Germany. *Sprechen sie Deutsch?*" I improvised rapidly, before he had a chance to remember that school wasn't in session yet. "I'm studying clarinet and ballet as well as my academic stuff. American schools are a lot easier than the ones in Frankfurt. The weather's a lot hotter, too. I hope this is the sort of thing you want to print in your paper."

All this stuff just leaped out of my mouth, glib as if I'd rehearsed it for weeks. I amazed myself. The reporter was amazed, too, for a second. He closed his mouth, which had fallen open, and then said, "Uh, but how is Mrs. Buechner taking the situation? Could I speak to her?"

I lost my temper. "It's pronounced Book-ner, not Betch-ner," I said very loudly. Then I turned and stomped down the driveway and into the house. I didn't exactly slam the door, because Mom was asleep. But I locked it as hard as I could and put the chain up, hoping the reporter could hear me doing it.

Inside, I moved around as quietly as possible, making a big pot of coffee and some toast. But Mrs. Doherty woke up, anyway. "Oh, good girl! Coffee's what I need."

"Wouldn't you rather lie down some more?" I suggested. "You could use my bed, there's another afghan somewhere."

117

"No, thank you, dear—I had a good nap on the sofa last night." She yawned. "Let your mother rest as long as possible. We can bring the little TV in here."

A quick scan of the TV channels showed that nobody ran news updates so early. Instead we read the *Post*. The State Department situation was the biggest story. There were maps of the relevant area of the city, and diagrams of the building. I didn't want to look at the photo of the man they had already shot. But I forced myself to read about it. Security guard Jim Farouk had been killed right at the beginning. I wondered if he had any children.

Most terrible of all, there was a photo of Dad under the gun. The caption read, "Hostage Donald Buechner and captor make a brief appearance at the 23rd Street entrance." Daddy's face was turned aside, but I knew him by his clothes. The terrorist was just barely visible in the gray shadows beyond him. The paper had marked a white circle around his head to show where he was.

I felt so depressed I couldn't go on to read the comics. I wished I were as young as Shannon, so that I could just cry and cry like she did. Or, if I were as old as Abe, I might have total self-control. Instead, I sat crumbling my toast into powder on my plate and quivering.

Abe stumped in and grabbed the front page. He sat down and frowned at my plate. "What a mess, Rianne!" he said, disgusted. "If you're not going to eat it, throw it out."

"There's a picture of Daddy in the paper," I said unsteadily.

118

Mrs. Doherty got up. "Who'd like some scrambled eggs?" she asked.

"I would, please," Abe said. Then, more quietly, he said to me, "If you're done, why don't you get on out back?"

I nodded and picked up my plate. After I put it into the sink, I scuffed into my sneakers and wandered casually out the back door.

Every day over the last two weeks had been hot and sunny. Today, when I had to go outdoors, the sky lowered with clouds as solid and dense as a white ceiling. The air dripped with moisture, and the grass shimmered with dew. Pretty soon it would rain.

When I peeked around the corner of the house I saw the white van still parked at the curb. On tiptoe I made my way down the hill. This time I resolved not to thrash though the undergrowth like a cow. If Robin Hood can walk through a forest quietly, why not me? I took it slowly, pushing past one thorny branch before attacking the next, and watching where I put my feet. There were no trails or paths once I passed the tot lot, or at least none that I could use—I suppose the rabbits and raccoons have their byways and roads. But there were always little open places where a tree root squeezed out other growth or where a sapling had blown over. Since I didn't much care which direction I went, I made pretty fair progress by following along these little openings.

A fine, misty rain began to fall, but I hardly got wet. When I looked up, I couldn't really see the sky. Leaves and boughs interlaced with more leaves and boughs overhead until only a few drops sifted through.

Suddenly through the trees I noticed a cleared place ahead, a big one. It hadn't been here last month. I made my way to the edge of the forest. Beyond, the land was unrecognizable—a wilderness of bare red mud bleeding into the gullies. A dozen raw cement foundations stuck up like broken teeth from the ooze. No workmen were there, I guess because it was Saturday, but some bright yellow tractors and machines were parked here and there. Winding away up the hill was a churned-up track that someday would be a road. Beside it was a big sign with ornate curly letters that read, HUNTLEIGH MEWS—FORTY EXCLUSIVE TOWNHOME RESIDENCES.

I flopped down onto a cut stump and began to cry. Of course I hadn't brought a hankie or even some Kleenex. I had to wipe my nose on the hem of my T-shirt. All the construction and machinery had surely driven the wildlife away. The Impossumble was gone. She might even be dead, bulldozed by a tractor or something. When I thought about the danger Daddy was in, and how he might be dying right now, I sobbed out loud. In a sense it was all my fault. I had found the Impossumble in the first place.

"What a horrible noise you make, almost as bad as a bulldozer," a small, rusty voice remarked. "Does it have any significance?"

And there was the Impossumble, perched comfortably on a fallen log. For the first time I lost patience with her. "Yes, it does!" I yelled. "It means that we're in the worst trouble you can imagine! And it's all your doing—we never would have accepted those 'bits of luck' if we'd known!" Then I leaned my head on my

knees and just howled. It was funny, how easy it had been to be polite when I didn't need anything from the Impossumble. Now I needed an important favor, and I yelled at her.

Surprisingly, the Impossumble took no offense at my outburst. "I suppose something nasty has happened to you," she said, in the voice of someone for whom pessimism is a way of life. "Maybe that boy was eaten by a fox?"

This suggestion was so ridiculous I stopped crying. "A lot of aggravating things," I sniffled. "But the most important is Daddy." There was, of course, no point in telling the Impossumble about the hostages or the State Department or firearms. "A trap, I guess you might call it," I tried to explain. "We're afraid he'll be killed."

"Too bad," the Impossumble said indifferently.

"Don't you understand?" I cried. "Something has to be done! Some luck has to be pushed his way!"

"It's not worth it. It never is." The Impossumble sounded a lot like Abe, with that maddening "I surely know better than you" tone. "Take my word for it, you'd just have twice as much trouble in the end."

"We want twice as much trouble," I said vehemently. "We want aggravation. Daddy's life is worth anything."

"I'm sure your father would disagree." The Impossumble seemed to be in even more contrary a mood than usual. "A parent would rather preserve her kits, or cubs, or children, or whatever. That's the natural order—the old die, and leave room for the young."

I realized that if I wanted the Impossumble to

cooperate I'd have to think of an answer to that. "But you're always saying people aren't natural," I said with an effort. "We're always doing unnatural things—building houses, riding bikes, cooking food."

"That's true," the Impossumble admitted. "All this politeness and kindness stuff is totally unanimal." She glowered at me, and all of a sudden it occurred to me that she was upset, too.

"How have you been, Impossumble?" I asked. "Do all these workmen bother you?"

"They didn't cut down *my* tree," the opossum grumped. "But they chopped down all the trees to one side of it. Now my wonderful, cozy, private hole faces right out over the building site. The noise is driving me mad!"

"Of course," I sympathized. "Since you sleep in your hole during the daytime the trucks must be very disturbing."

"Exactly." Having someone to discuss the problem with seemed to be some comfort. "I just hope they'll pack up their disgusting, smelly machines come winter, and go away."

"But, Impossumble," I said. "Don't you know they're building houses?"

"They *are*?" the Impossumble almost screamed.

I pointed at the sign. "Forty of them, it says there."

"Forty!" The Impossumble's eyes glowed red. "I can't live near *forty* people." She bared her teeth at me, as if it were all my fault. "I suppose they'll have cars!"

"I'm pretty sure of it," I said. "And tricycles, and playgrounds, and lawn sprinklers, and basketball hoops." A tremendous idea had burst into my mind, and I piled on the woe. "They'll have barbecue grills that they'll light over the weekends. And I guess they'll mow their lawns a lot. And put out their trash twice a week. There'll be garbage trucks, and mail trucks, and moving vans, and ice-cream men—"

The Impossumble hid her head between her paws as if to shut out the sight of all these intruders. "I can't bear it. I'll have to move!"

"Where to?"

"I don't know." She gnashed her white sharp teeth at me. "There are people *everywhere*. You're a worse plague than gypsy moths."

"You know," I said, as if the idea had just occurred to me, "there's a big nature center near here. The woods there are protected by the community. I'll bet all the animals there live in peace and quiet."

"They do?"

"I might be willing to take you there, and your stuff too, on my bike," I pursued. "As a favor to a friend. And maybe you could give a little push to Daddy's luck."

The Impossumble shook herself briskly. "If you'll take me to safety I'd be glad to! If you want to suffer aggravation and trouble, that's your problem."

"Oh, thank you, Impossumble," I said, leaping up. I could have hugged her, but remembered that a wild animal would never let a human touch her.

"Your luck is more off balance than ever, now," the Impossumble warned again.

"I don't care," I said, dancing like a top. "I'll park my bike at the edge of our yard. You can put anything you want to bring in the basket tonight."

"And where will I ride?" the Impossumble demanded morosely.

"Shannon will come too, and you can ride with her. See you tomorrow!" And I set off up the hill as fast as I could.

Unfortunately, I was so happy I didn't watch where I was going. I reached to steady myself on a branch, and my hand broke through something hard and papery. Suddenly a cloud of wasps surrounded me, buzzing like chainsaws. I screamed and ran, blundering through the bushes. I got half a dozen stings before I broke out of the woods.

By the time I reached the back door I was crying again from the pain. Thank goodness Mom was up! She swatted the wasps that had swarmed through the door after me, and then made a paste of baking soda to spread on the stings. "Now there's nothing to cry about anymore, darling," she comforted me, and passed a box of tissues.

"What about Dad?" I managed to choke.

Before she could answer Abe yelled from the living room. "Mom! They've sent in the SWAT team!"

"Oh, dear Lord!" Mom almost spilled the baking soda as she jumped up.

As we gathered around the TV tension ran so high I could taste it. Both TVs were on, and the radio too, but all we saw was commercials. Then suddenly the news flashed on. Policemen ran by in bulky bulletproof clothes and blue helmets, shiny-round like Christmas balls. The big glass doors crashed into heaps of splinters. I would have thought they would just shoot the glass out with their guns, but the explosives squad used shaped charges. Then they all raced inside.

"I don't see Daddy," Shannon whimpered.

We all groaned as a commercial for dog food came on. "I'll never buy Puppy Snax, as long as I live," Mrs. Doherty vowed.

Abe stood up. "Rianne, can you help me get some ice?"

"Sure." I knew what he really wanted. As soon as we got to the kitchen I said, "The Impossumble has fixed it, but we'll have mounds more bad luck to make up for Dad's escape. That's how I got these awful stings."

"Never mind the stings, it'll be worth it." Abe held the freezer door open while I scooped ice out. "Unless—"

"Unless what?"

"Well, what if that isn't enough? Or if we're too late?"

I remembered how I had loitered over breakfast out of pure laziness, and how I had wandered slowly through the woods, and the tears rushed to my eyes again.

"Oh, don't cry again, Ree, please." Abe watched my face nervously. "Everything we could do, we did."

We sat in front of the TV for what could have been hours, but was actually about forty minutes. Then a police spokesman came on, grinning all over his face, to announce a successful rescue. "Among the freed are Randall Portin, Lynnette Gray, Donald Buechner—"

"Oh, hooray!" "Thank God!" we cheered. Mom

burst into tears of relief. Abe blew his nose on a tissue. I hugged Shannon, who cried like a sponge. Mrs. Doherty kissed us all and announced, "Now I'm going to cook the poor man a nice dinner!"

Dad came home that evening at the usual time. He didn't look usual, though, all tired and dirty, with his yellow mustache straggling and his chin bristly. A State Department car brought him back. Shannon and I raced up the driveway to meet him, yelling and whooping. Close behind us came Mom. Abe brought up the rear, hopping along on his good foot like a kangaroo and waving his crutches. The white van had been joined by some cars and a camera crew, but nobody cared.

We leaped on Daddy all together and hugged whatever bits of him we could reach. Mom wiped her tears on Dad's wrinkled and sweat-stained shirtfront. Shannon used his back pockets and his belt as footholds to climb up his back, something she's really too big now to try. Luckily, she was able to get up and hug Dad's neck before his pants pockets tore out. Daddy hugged and kissed us all. Finally, when Abe nearly beaned me by accident with a crutch, Dad said, "Okay, calm down, troops! Let's go inside before you wrestle me to the ground."

As we turned to go back down to the house, the reporters moved in. "Can we take a picture of you and your family, Mr. Buechner?" a photographer called.

"Sure," Dad said. "I'm in a very good mood." He hugged me with one arm and Mom with the other, while Abe towered to one side and Shannon stood in front. I saw the newsman from this morning looking at me oddly, but I was too happy to mind. The reporters' interest didn't seem nosy or intrusive anymore, and I realized how much my own feelings had colored how they looked to me.

"Home at last!" Dad exclaimed, as he stepped through the door. Mrs. Doherty had left after making a tremendous beef stew. "My tummy is flapping against my spine," Dad sighed happily, as we sat down to it.

"I peeled the potatoes and carrots," Shannon said.

"And I vacuumed the downstairs while Mom took a nap," I added.

"I'm very proud of you all," Dad said, and yawned—he hadn't slept last night at all. "That's what makes a house a home."

14

The following day Abe and I corralled Shannon out on the deck after breakfast, and explained everything. "We've got to be very, very careful for a while," I said.

"Better a dozen minor disasters than one big tragedy," Abe agreed.

"But can we do that?" Shannon was dubious. "Have broken ankles instead of auto accidents, I mean."

"How would I know? All we can do is try it. And a bum ankle is *not* what I mean when I say minor. The injury will probably affect my game for the rest of my life!" Although he knows it's not of the *first* importance, Abe still feels we should treat his sprain with respect.

"But it's hard to think what we can do," I said.

"Let's make Daddy get a safer job," Shannon proposed.

I scratched at my wasp stings. "I think that two hostage incidents so soon would be pretty unlikely," I said.

"Besides, how could we make him do it? We have to watch out for other things." Abe hoisted his leg up to rest on the railing, and right away Jane climbed into the newly created lap. "I'll tell you what—let's get the folks to have both cars serviced and tuned up."

"Good idea!" I applauded. "And I saw in the paper that the police department will come around to inspect your house for security hazards. Let's call them."

"And Jane should get some shots," Shannon suggested. "Feline leukemia and rabies."

It seemed we were really getting a handle on the problem. The bad thing about this kind of approach is that you begin to feel secure. When Shannon caught her finger in the sliding door as we went in, it was a shock. All the skin was scraped off her knuckle. She bled like a pig, and screamed like one, too. Mom was so busy bandaging it that the pot roast, which was supposed to be getting brown on the stove, burnt black. "Ten dollars' worth of meat gone," she sighed. "Oh, well."

I was afraid Shannon would be too upset to bike with me to the nature center, but she said she was okay. From pure nervous exhaustion we had slept pretty late that morning, and missed church. When Shannon and I went down to the backyard, the Impossumble was waiting for us. "Where have you been?" she snapped, her naked pink tail quivering with impatience. "The sun's been up for hours!"

"We had a little accident," I said, kicking up the stand of my bike. "Are you all loaded up?"

My bike basket was full of what looked like dried leaves and trash. But the Impossumble said, "Yes, you have all my valuables there. So go carefully!"

"Come on up to the driveway," Shannon said, very

anxious to be polite, "and you can get into my basket. I have a nice grocery bag there for you to ride in, and an apple. Is that okay?"

"I suppose," the Impossumble said grudgingly.

"It'll be just like taking an airplane," I said. "An in-flight snack and deluxe seating."

We laid the bag in the driveway, and the Impossumble climbed into it. Then I lifted it gently into Shannon's handlebar basket. The paper bag had been my

idea. It would have been pretty conspicious to tool around with a wild animal sitting in plain view on the front of her bike.

We set off down the bike trail. It had rained off and on all night, and a high, cluttery handful of clouds was still visible away to the west. The woods gleamed wet and fresh after all that rain. I had never bicycled to the nature center before, but we had passed it once in the car. Unlike the main roads, though, the trail system doesn't have a lot of signs. We took a wrong turn and wound up clear down at the high school. Then we had to backtrack, so the trip took almost an hour.

At the edge of several acres of preserved woodland was the nature center building. It was a small, square pavilion with pointed angles on the roof like slices of cake. There were picnic tables scattered around, and the bulletin board on the side of the building carried a list of the programs offered—nature hikes, animal observation tours, and so on. Since it was Sunday there were no programs scheduled. Two or three cars parked in the small parking lot showed that a few people were there—hikers and fanatic birdwatchers, probably. We wheeled our bikes around to the back of the building, out of casual view.

I lifted the grocery bag out carefully and set it on the ground. The Impossumble crept out, groaning. "Oh, I feel dreadfully ill! All the bouncing and swaying . . ."

She lay down on the gravel and curled her nose into her gray belly fur. "You didn't eat your apple," Shannon said, looking into the bag.

"It'll soon pass," I tried to comfort the Impossumble. "Just a little motion sickness, that's all."

"Would a bite of apple help?" Shannon offered, but the Impossumble turned away in disgust.

"If you hadn't just done me an important favor I would hit you with the worst luck you ever saw," she snarled weakly.

Shannon looked so scared and worried I had to say, "But that would ensure some really good luck later on, wouldn't it?"

"Don't argue with me," the Impossumble growled. "We animals never worry about the future, anyway. Except for winter. You can pile all my stuff over there, behind that big clump of grass. I'll move it to my new nest, when I find one, bit by bit."

Most of the Impossumble's baggage looked like nothing in particular—leaves, a bit of gnarled wood, some walnut shells, and an old, dry peach pit. She had brought her handkerchief comforter, but it was pretty grimy now. We emptied everything out of the basket, including every single dry leaf, and stacked it carefully where she had told us to. "Well, I guess we won't see you much anymore," I said a little uncertainly.

"I hope not," the Impossumble said crossly. "I'm going *deep* into this forest, so I'll never see a person again."

I was a little sorry to hear this, but much more relieved. In theory, all the good things the Impossumble had brought us were exactly outweighed by bad. But after Daddy's experience I knew we'd never tinker with our luck again. "Oh, but I'll miss you," Shannon said—a dumb comment under the circumstances! "Have—have a good life!"

"Yes, keep yourself safe," I said.

"Of course I will," the Impossumble said in a huff, as if I had implied she was incompetent to do so. She shambled off towards the trees. "Well—good-bye."

"Good-bye!" "Good-bye!"

"Oh—" The Impossumble turned back at the edge of the woods. "Thank you," she said, so reluctantly you would have thought we were pulling out her teeth. Then she scuttled off into the underbrush.

Shannon breathed a long sigh of relief mingled with regret. "She's really gone!"

"I guess so."

"And we'll never see her again?"

"You know," I said thoughtfully, "she said once that it wasn't really good for us to associate with her. And I think she's right."

Shannon picked up the bag and the apple. "Shall I leave the apple with her stuff?"

"Sure, why not. With luck the Impossumble will come back for her things before the squirrels find it."

"If there's anybody who has luck, it's the Impossumble," Shannon declared.

On Wednesday we noticed the lawn was turning brown. The garden equivalent of the bubonic plague swept over the grass that Abe and Dad had sweated over. In a few days it looked like the Gobi Desert. All the brown, dry grass lay flat on the ground as if it couldn't even muster the strength to die standing up. People walking by with their dogs would stare and drag their animals over to the far side, in case it was catching. Disgusted, Dad swore he would pave it over with asphalt and paint it green.

Thursday, the air conditioner made a peculiar clanking noise and stopped dead. For a few hours in the morning, we went around repeating to each other that people survive all the time without air-conditioning. It was a brutally hot day, without a cloud in the sky. The forecast was for temperatures in the high nineties, with seventy percent humidity. When the repairman said he couldn't fix it that day, Mom blew her top. She made him promise, cross his heart, to fix it Friday morning. And he did, too. When Mom resorts to that tone of voice, everybody hops.

That weekend was the Labor Day holiday. Unanimously, we kids said we didn't want to drive to the beach. We didn't want to see the pandas at the zoo. We didn't want to go to the lake and rent a boat. The folks were kind of surprised, after all our whining about being bored. "We just want to stay quietly at home with you, Daddy," Shannon said, cuddling her head into his arm.

If I try soft soap like that, Dad always can tell, but as the baby of the family Shannon gets away with it. "We'll have a nice old-fashioned cookout instead," Mom promised.

We went with Dad to the grocery store, where he chose a big, thick porterhouse steak for each of us. Slabs of red meat and pizza are the only foods Dad claims to be expert on. This time he made a big production of it, looking over all the plastic-wrapped packages carefully. He lighted the charcoal in the grill and then left Mom to decide when it was hot enough to start cooking the steaks. She was out on the deck fiddling with them when there came a tremendous boom. I looked out my bedroom window and saw a fountain of fire shooting up, like an exploding volcano. We ran out to the deck and found Mom sitting on the planks with her face all black and her eyebrows burnt off. Her glasses had been blown off her nose and over the edge of the deck, where they lay unbroken down below in a thick tuft of dead brown grass. A circular column of flame was blasting straight up from the grill and crisping the leaves that overhung the deck. It looked unreal, like a special effect in a Spielberg movie. Daddy grabbed the kitchen fire extinguisher and sprayed the grill. The fountain of flame vanished instantly, and a strong chemical smell filled the air.

"The charcoal wasn't burning very well," Mom explained in a weak voice. "So I squirted on some more lighter fluid."

"Of all the boneheaded things to do, Irene!" Dad was really mad. "When it says right there on the label not to do that! It's a mercy you weren't seriously burned!"

Mom swabbed at the greasy smut on her face with a paper towel. "I didn't think," she admitted. "Pure carelessness, you're right. Oh dear, my poor eyebrows! We'll have to buy another grill."

Shannon skittered down to the lawn to fetch Mom's glasses. Abe hobbled cautiously closer to the grill, and stared at the steaks. "Even Jane won't eat those," he said sadly. The meat was black and crisp like cinders, and speckled with white foam from the fire extinguisher. The grill was all twisted and blasted looking from the explosion. No one felt like barbecuing any more. We went in and heated up a casserole from the freezer for dinner.

What Mom said brought another nasty thought to mind. All these aggravations weren't just annoying. They were pretty expensive. It weighed on me so much I brought up the subject obliquely with Dad, as I helped him drag the twisted grill to the curb for the trash men to take away. "Are we going to be really poor, Daddy?"

He laughed gently at me, and I felt better. "I think the family finances can handle buying another grill, Rianne. This time maybe a kettle grill, so that if your mother gets creative with charcoal lighter fluid again we can just clap the lid on."

"But what about everything else? The new ceiling, repairing the roof, the new car—"

Dad looked at me. "That's the first time I've heard you worrying about the budget."

"It's just that there's been so *much* happening," I said vaguely.

We walked back down the driveway, and Dad hugged my shoulders with a big strong hand. "It hasn't been the most pleasant summer," he agreed. "But life is like that, Rianne. There are ups and downs every year. Just like there are always waves going up and down in the ocean. We have to learn to steam on through, and not let them push us off course."

"But we haven't been exactly, uh, *lucky*," I said.

"Luck is relative, Rianne. Like the days of the week. People agree to have seven days in a week, but there's no intrinsic reason to do so—not the way you definitely have to have day and night, for instance."

"I don't see how you can say that, Daddy," I argued. "You were really lucky last weekend—nothing relative about it!"

We sat down together on the front stoop. Now that the day was almost over, it was cool enough to be comfortable out front. "Well, that's a good example," Dad said. "I was lucky to get out. But unlucky to have gotten captured. But lucky not to have been shot right off . . . A lot of the time you can make your own luck by perseverance and hard work."

"Like Mom getting accepted by the masters program?" I asked, enlightened.

"Sure—she worked hard, and dreamed, and planned, to achieve that. If she hadn't put in all the work it never would have come her way, luck or no."

What I admire most about Dad is the way he can *cope*. I resolved that if it killed me I would learn to cope, too. This horrible time would pass. The Impossumble had said so. And in the meantime I refused to let it get me down.

It was good that I had decided that, because the bad luck wasn't done yet. On Sunday, while we were at church, Jane went out and had a tremendous fight with some new cat. We came home to find her sitting on the door mat with her left ear in ribbons. Blood dripped into the short fur on her head, and when she shook her head it spattered all over the door, the front stoop, and our good Sunday clothes.

"Oh! We have to do something, she'll bleed to death!" Shannon's marshmallow-soft heart actually would make her a pretty poor vet. She knelt beside Jane and wrung her hands, not daring to touch her.

138

Jane mewed piteously. She knew she needed help. I was proud of her intelligence. "I'll get a box from the basement," I volunteered.

"Change your clothes first," Mom said.

"But Mom, what if Jane runs away?" Tears began to run down Shannon's cheeks. "Then she might *die*."

"We'll be careful and quick, Mom," I promised. And in fact Jane felt so ill she didn't fight being boxed at all. We hurried into our jeans while Abe phoned around to find a vet who would see an emergency on Labor Day weekend.

From the car Dad called, "Well, where is it?"

"The only one is in Sterling, Dad," I said breathlessly, as I got into the car. I handed him the address on a piece of paper. "On Conte Road. She'll be expecting us."

"Wonderful," Dad said gloomily. "Get out the street map, Shannon."

As soon as the engine started, Jane began to yowl. She really doesn't approve of riding in cars. The sound was incredible, like having a power saw screaming next to your ear. Jane didn't even seem to stop to take a breath. Shannon had to shout the directions to Dad, while I sat in back holding the box. Remembering Jane's last car trip, I was very careful to keep the box flaps down tight.

Whether because of Shannon's map reading, or whether Dad couldn't hear well—or maybe because all the new construction around the town of Sterling has turned the street signs around—we got lost. We drove round and round for ages, until Dad lost his patience and pulled over to look at the map himself.

There was no Conte Road on it. We asked at a gas station, where they didn't know, either. At last Dad had to phone the vet again to get exact directions. It was pathetic.

Poor Jane had to have stitches, which took some time. We hadn't had time for lunch, so while Jane was in the vet's office Dad took us to a burger joint. We didn't get home until almost dinnertime. "An entire afternoon shot with that cat," Dad said in a tight voice. "I was hoping to get in a few licks on that lawn today."

Monday, Labor Day itself, started badly too. The toaster quietly broke, and burned Abe's toast. Abe has the unnatural gift of getting up very early, well before seven. He'd gotten into the habit in Manila, when the only comfortable time to play tennis is early. This morning the burning toast set off the smoke detector. A piercing hoot jerked everyone up out of sound sleep. We staggered out into the hall, rubbing our eyes and mumbling questions. Dad went downstairs and took the battery out of the detector. "Go back to sleep, Irene," he said as he came back up the stairs.

"After that?" Mom yawned. "You're kidding."

Shannon followed me back to my room. "Rianne, school starts tomorrow."

The prospect was a scary one, but I wasn't going to admit it. "So what?'

"Oh, Rianne, what if we're still such horrible jinxes?"

"There's nothing we can do about it but tough it out. Now shove, runt. I want to get dressed."

Even Abe seemed depressed by the idea of starting out in a new school under a cloud like this. "We have to keep on telling ourselves that any amount of annoyance is better than losing Mom or Dad," he said after breakfast.

"Tell that to Shannon," I snapped.

"Someday, sometime, it'll be over," Abe insisted. "Our luck debts will be paid off."

"How will we know when it happens?" I couldn't help asking, even though I knew Abe was just trying to be encouraging. "We're not going to get a bank statement in the mail, like with MasterCard."

"Well, something good will happen, some stroke of luck."

"I'm so sick of that word," I declared. "After this summer, I never want to hear it again!"

It throws my whole day off to be waked up so early. I sat in the living room and watched the cartoons on TV, and just gloomed. I could imagine all the dreadful things that might happen tomorrow. Maybe the school had lost my transcript. My locker might jam. The automatic sprinkler system might go off and get me soaking wet. Probably both the air conditioner and heating system would break. I wouldn't be able to find my school bus. Everything looked overcast up ahead, with no hope of a sunnier forecast. For the hundredth time I wished we had stayed in Manila.

I couldn't stand cartoons anymore, so I went out into the front yard. Glancing up and down the block, I saw that our lawn was the only one on Hartwick Road that looked like a quarter of an acre of doormat.

It was like the mark of Zorro or something, branding us as jinxes. I bent to look at the grass closely, but it looked absolutely dead.

"There's one, I can see it coming up." Someone spoke right behind me and I jumped.

"What's coming up?"

"The autumn crocuses," she said. A tall, thin girl stood on our driveway, pointing. She had curly brown hair cut short all over, like a poodle's fur. Her bare, knobbly knees, very tan, stuck out from under her shorts. Her thin face was long too, rather like a horse's, but I liked the look of it right away. "Hi— you don't know me, but I'm Louise DeConcino, from next door."

For a second I had to think. "Oh, you're Mrs. Hernandez's granddaughter!"

"That's right. You've never seen this yard in September, have you? There are about a million colchicums, or whatever they are, planted in there. It looks like a flower show when they all bloom."

"You're kidding." I stared hard at the space between the dry, dead grass and the bushes. Sure enough, there were dozens of little white points sticking up, like baby pencils. "And I thought this yard would always look like the Curse of the Cantervilles."

She laughed and said, "I read that story. Listen, could my folks come over later today and meet your folks?"

"Sure, I guess. What for, just to get acquainted?"

"Well, that too. But Mom is really upset about the tree falling on your house. You see she'd really meant to have it cut down in the spring, but the twins got

142

chicken pox and she never got around to it before we left."

I grinned. "Actually, now that I think back, it was kind of fun."

She grinned too. "Well, don't tell that to Mom. Her idea is that, to make up for all the hassle you were put to, we could lend you our vacation condo for a week, maybe over Christmas. It's in Orlando."

"You mean—Disney World?" My heart seemed to jump for joy in my chest. "Wow! But—wouldn't *you* want to use it?"

She rolled her eyes. "We've just come back from two weeks there. You know my little brothers, Brian and Billy? Well, you will. They're hellions. Two weeks in Disney World with *them*—" She stuck her tongue out and pretended to shudder. "Even my parents said enough is enough."

"I don't know what the folks'd say. But it sounds great to me! Thanks a whole bunch!"

"Are your folks up? Then let me go tell Mom to come over."

"Come on back after, and we'll have some lemonade," I invited her. "I'd love to hear about Venezuela."

"That's right, you've lived overseas too!"

"In Manila," I said. "Where were you in Venezuela, in Caracas?"

"I wish! No, Daddy's a botanist. We were near Puerto Ayacucho, on the Orinoco River right in the jungle. It was the pits. You have no idea how good it is to be back in Reston."

I had never imagined anyone could feel that way.

143

"It'll sure give you something to tell at school, when they ask you what you did this summer."

"Yeah—I'll show you my machete, it's cool. You pour that lemonade—I'll be right back, after I tell Mom."

She trotted off across to her house. I sat down limply on the front step, too happy to stand up any more. Even the dry, brown lawn looked like it might be greening up a little, down at the roots. Behind me, Abe hobbled to the screen door. "I thought of something good that'll happen, Ree. I get my cast off this week."

"That's right, you do! But I can top that—I just met our next-door neighbor. We steamed on through the bad time, just like Dad said. The luck has turned, Abe! Happy days are here again!"